Logan knew Abby was upset with him again.

He gave up with a sigh. When she got her dander up, there was no reasoning with her. She had slowed down the car a bit, a frown on her face. He thought of how careful his mother was never to create wrinkles. She stayed in the shade and applied cream to her face religiously.

Yet Abby's skin, with its light tan, looked soft and smooth. Touchable.

He stiffened at that thought. He was forgetting she was his boss. For a month. If she could read his mind, he'd be off the ranch in the blink of an eye.

Or she would be wrapped in his arms....

On sale June 2000: NEVER LET YOU GO
(Silhouette Romance #1453)
On sale July 2000: THE BORROWED GROOM
(Silhouette Romance #1457)
On sale August 2000: CHERISH THE BOSS
(Silhouette Romance #1463)

Dear Reader,

Though August is already upon us, we've got yet another month of special 20th anniversary titles sure to prolong your summer reading pleasure.

STORKVILLE, USA, our newest in-line continuity, launches this month with Marie Ferrarella's *Those Matchmaking Babies*. In this four-book series, the discovery of twin babies abandoned on a day care center's doorstep leads to secrets being revealed…and unsuspecting townsfolk falling in love!

Judy Christenberry rounds up THE CIRCLE K SISTERS with *Cherish the Boss*, in which an old-school cowboy and a modern woman find themselves at odds—and irresistibly attracted to each other! In Cara Colter's memorable VIRGIN BRIDES offering, the "world's oldest living virgin" meets the man she hopes will be her *First Time, Forever.*

Valerie Parv's THE CARRAMER CROWN continues, as a woman long in love with Michel de Marigny poses as *The Prince's Bride-To-Be.* Arlene James delights with *In Want of a Wife,* the story of a self-made millionaire who is looking for a mother for his adopted daughter—and, could it be, a wife for himself? And Natalie Patrick offers the charming *His, Hers…Ours?*, in which a marriage-wary pair play parents and discover they like it—and each other—far too much.

Next month, look for another installment of STORKVILLE, USA, and the launch of THE CHANDLERS REQUEST…from *New York Times* bestselling author Kasey Michaels.

Happy Reading!

Mary-Theresa Hussey

Mary-Theresa Hussey
Senior Editor

Please address questions and book requests to:
Silhouette Reader Service
U.S.: 3010 Walden Ave., P.O. Box 1325, Buffalo, NY 14269
Canadian: P.O. Box 609, Fort Erie, Ont. L2A 5X3

Cherish
the Boss

JUDY CHRISTENBERRY

Silhouette

ROMANCE™

Published by Silhouette Books
America's Publisher of Contemporary Romance

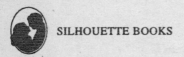

SILHOUETTE BOOKS

ISBN 0-373-19463-3

CHERISH THE BOSS

Visit Silhouette at www.eHarlequin.com

Printed in U.S.A.

Books by Judy Christenberry

Silhouette Romance

*Lucky Charm Sisters
†The Circle K Sisters

JUDY CHRISTENBERRY

has been writing romances for fifteen years because she loves happy endings as much as her readers do. She's a bestselling author for Harlequin American Romance, but she has a long love of traditional romances and is delighted to tell a story that brings those elements to the reader. A former high school French teacher, Judy now devotes her time to writing. She hopes readers have as much fun reading her stories as she does writing them. She spends her spare time reading, watching her favorite sports teams and keeping track of her two adult daughters.

Chapter One

"**D**on't move, darlin'," a soft masculine voice muttered behind Abigail Kennedy's back.

Her hands trembling, Abby lowered the barrel of the pistol she held so that it pointed toward the ground. She might as well, since it had no bullets left.

Her gaze remained fixed on what had been terrorizing her for the past few minutes.

A huge diamondback rattler.

A loud report sounded just behind her. Almost simultaneously, its head flew from its body.

With a gasp, she sank to her knees.

"You okay?" the voice asked. Warm hands clasped her shaking shoulders, lifting her to her feet again.

"I—I'm fine," she muttered, embarrassed by her behavior. She felt as if she should wear a placard around her neck: Terrorized By Snakes. It made her feel weak and silly and—and horrible. "Thank you for killing it."

"My pleasure," he said, reaching around her for her pistol.

Abby whirled away from him, clutching the gun.

Her rescuer backed away, his hands, one still clutching a rifle, raised in the air. "Hey, darlin', I was just going to take the gun before you accidentally shot yourself."

Abby stared at him. He was the perfect hero. Tall, broad-shouldered, his smooth features Hollywood perfect. She never trusted a handsome man.

"It's not loaded," she muttered, glaring at him.

His firm but sensual mouth kicked up at one corner. "Hell, no wonder you hadn't killed that varmint."

She had to be honest, even though it shamed her. "It had bullets. I—I shot them all."

"I thought I heard some shooting." He peered around her at what was left of the snake, its body still twitching. She knew what he saw. No bullet holes.

He cleared his throat. "Maybe you'd better consider doing some target practicing. I could give you a few pointers."

"No, thank you," she said, her voice crisp with rejection. She had great marksmanship. It was the snake that caused the problem. She had an irrational terror of them.

One eyebrow shot up, but his only response was a nod. Then he asked, "What are you doing way out here?"

Since Abby was on the family ranch, the one she

had run for the past seven or eight years, she found his question bizarre. "You're asking *me* what I'm doing out here?"

He gave her a cocky cowboy grin. "Well, darlin', I don't see anyone else I could be talking to."

"First of all," she explained, her voice tight, "my name is not darlin'. Second, you're trespassing. I think that question should be directed at you, not me."

"Well now, I don't mind answering, but I'm not trespassing. I'm an invited guest."

"Invited by whom?"

His eyebrows soared again, drawing attention to his hazel eyes. Yes, the man was definitely impressive. But Abby refused to be moved. Even if she did owe him for killing the snake.

She didn't like his attitude.

"By the owner, Miss Abigail Kennedy. The old lady wants to hire me as her manager."

"Oh, really?" So this was Logan Crawford, late of Oklahoma. Well, she'd made a mistake. She wouldn't be hiring this man. "I don't think that's going to happen."

"Don't tell me. I'm talking to the boss's daughter? Don't I get points for saving your life?" He gestured to the snake.

Abby couldn't hold back a shudder. Nor could she dismiss some gratitude. But hiring this man as manager would never work. "Yes. But I'm not the boss's daughter. Abigail Kennedy isn't married."

He studied her, his hazel gaze traveling over her, and Abby could almost feel that look. But she didn't back away. Standing her ground, she waited until he'd taken inventory. A very detailed inventory.

"Finished?" she drawled, letting him know she didn't appreciate his appraisal.

"Yes, ma'am," he assured her, his mouth tilting up in a sexy grin. "They sure grow 'em fine here in Texas."

"Grow what fine?" She gritted her teeth waiting for his answer.

"Ladies. You're a beautiful woman. But you probably need a tad more common sense. It's not smart to be riding alone."

Now it wasn't impatience or dislike that filled her. It was plain old anger. She admitted to having a temper, but she normally kept it under strict control. "So you always work with a partner?"

"I try to. It makes good sense."

"Well, thanks for the advice, Mr. Crawford. Now, I apologize for your long drive, but I don't think things are going to work out. I'll be glad to reimburse you for your trouble."

The smiling flirtatiousness left his face and his hazel eyes narrowed, still focused on her. "You're Abigail Kennedy?"

"Yes. The 'old lady,' herself." She enjoyed the surprise he showed.

"But I understood—my father said the owner was in her seventies."

"She was," Abby said, drawing a deep breath, "until she died about eighteen months ago."

Logan Crawford sighed. He hadn't done enough research. When his father had told him about the

Kennedy spread, he'd taken his word for the fact that Abigail Kennedy was the original owner, a woman in her seventies.

He'd assumed he'd be running a ranch for a woman well past her prime, unable to even supervise his work.

Not that he was concerned about supervision. He knew the job and did it well. But he liked a free hand.

This woman was a different matter.

She was dressed like a cowboy, tight jeans, a plaid shirt, leather gloves, a Stetson and, of course, boots. When he'd heard the gunfire, he'd hurried over, sure someone was in trouble.

It had taken him a minute to figure out that someone was a woman. When she'd turn to face him, there was no doubt. Flat-chested she wasn't. Besides, there was a sweetness to her features, a fullness in her lips, that proclaimed woman.

But his boss?

Then he remembered she'd just dismissed him. "Not planning on that interview you promised me?"

Her cheeks flushed, letting him know she realized she wasn't being fair. "I don't think it's necessary. Our personalities don't mesh."

"Darlin', I'm not here to take tea with you every day. My job would be out on the spread, working with your hands. I know the business."

And he wanted this job. Not because he was broke and desperate. Not because he'd been fired from his last job. Not even because he was nursing a broken heart and wanted a change of scenery.

He wanted this job because it would be a challenge. Because he wanted to determine if he liked the area before he invested his money in his own place. Because he had to get away from his brothers before they drove him crazy.

"I'm sure you do know the business, Mr. Crawford. Your résumé was impressive."

Nice words, but she said them dismissively.

"Then why don't I get to have an interview?"

She lifted her chin and faced him, but after a second she looked away. Then she said, "Because it would be a waste of time. I'll write you a check for your expenses."

She started walking away from him, and he frowned, realizing he was going to have to give up his plans. Then she came to an abrupt halt.

"What is it?" he asked, watching her.

"I, um, I—how did you get here?"

"My horse. I left him over there, in the trees," he said. He hadn't wanted to announce his presence until he'd figured out what was going on.

"Oh."

"What?"

"I thought maybe you'd driven."

It suddenly occurred to him that she *didn't* have a horse in sight. Or a truck. She was stranded.

The situation tickled his sense of humor. "I declare, Miss Kennedy, I do believe I'm going to have the opportunity to rescue you a second time today."

Her cheeks flooded with color and he admired her beautiful skin. Even in masculine dress, she was quite a beauty. And proud. She raised her chin. "I'll meet you at the house, but it will take me a while to get there.''

With that comment she started walking.

He chuckled, then crossed over to the trees to Dusty, his sorrel gelding, one of his favorite mounts. Swinging into the saddle, he replaced his rifle in the saddle holster and rode to her side. ''Come on. I'll give you a lift.''

''No, thank you.''

He scratched the back of his neck. She was a stubborn lady. But then, he could be stubborn, too.

He followed her across the pasture before he realized he had the key to her surrender.

''Good thing you have on boots,'' he said with a smile. ''They'll protect you if you run across any more rattlers.''

Hiding his smile, he watched as she froze, staring at the grass around her, as if a snake were behind every blade.

She stared at him. ''That was mean.''

''Yeah, I know. But it is a possibility. And you walking all the way back to the homestead is ridiculous when I've offered you a ride.''

With an abrupt nod, she turned to him. ''All right, I'll accept your offer.''

Kicking his left boot out of the stirrup, he ordered, ''Throw your leg over the saddle horn. Riding up front will be more comfortable.''

''No. I'll ride behind you.'' She took the hand he offered, put her foot in the stirrup and swung up behind him.

He admired her athletic ability. ''What happened to your mount?''

"The snake scared her. I—I wasn't paying attention and she dumped me and headed for the house."

He frowned. "I didn't see her on my way."

"Ellen probably directed you through the gates," she explained, naming her housekeeper. "Ruby jumps fences. I'm sure she went home by a more direct route."

"Hmm. Dusty doesn't mind fences. Want to go home the same way?" he asked, already knowing her answer.

"Not unless you want to give me my second dumping at the first fence. I don't think riding double and jumping fences go together."

With a chuckle, he clicked to Dusty to start him moving again. With a small gasp, the woman behind him grabbed his belt.

"Why don't you put your arms around my waist? You'll feel more secure."

She didn't answer. Then, when he'd decided she was going to be stubborn again, slim arms wrapped around him and a very definitely feminine body pressed against his back. He took a deep breath.

Keep your mind on business, he reminded himself. The ride back to the house was going to be his only opportunity to interview for a job he'd decided would be perfect for him. Except for one thing.

"Uh, I've had a lot of experience with Herefords," he said, naming the type of cow the Circle K ran.

"Yes, so your résumé indicated."

He wished he could see her face. "I was born on a ranch in Oklahoma and lived there most of my life. My dad was a tough taskmaster, teaching me every aspect of ranch life.''

''I know.''

Well, so far he was striking out. With a disgruntled huff, he tried one more time. ''I did save your life.''

''Why do you want to work here?''

Ah. The one thing he hadn't told her in the letters they'd exchanged. He hated to go into personal history, since he didn't think it applied to his ability to do the job, but he had no choice now.

''Miss Kennedy, I've got four brothers. The oldest, Joe, runs the ranch now. The next in line, Pete, handles the cattle. My brother Rick works with the horses. My little brother, Mike, is studying to be a lawyer. He doesn't want to be a cowboy.''

She said nothing.

With a sigh, he added, ''There's nothing left for me to do. No decisions to make. No chances to try my wings. I know the work. I love it. I want to run my own place.''

''But this is my place, Mr. Crawford.''

The words were soft but firm.

''I know that. I'd work within your guidelines, of course, but I could use my abilities without one of my brothers watching over my shoulder.''

They rode along in silence.

Finally he said, ''I don't reckon you have any brothers, Miss Kennedy, or you wouldn't be out by yourself, but do you have sisters?''

''Two sisters.''

''Well, think about how you'd feel if they were constantly watching over your shoulder, wanting to tell you how to do your work, even though you know perfectly well how it should be done.''

"So you want to get away from your family?"

"That's why this job is perfect for me. I want to get away, but not too far. Our place is about a two-hour drive from here. Close enough to visit, but impossible to supervise from." He chuckled as he remembered his brothers' reaction to his plan.

At least his father had understood and approved.

Abby couldn't help feeling sympathy for the man. Not that her sisters behaved that way. She loved her sisters. When their parents had been killed in a car accident when they were children, they'd clung to each other, drawing closer than ever.

Social Services had intended to split them up, put them in separate homes, when Aunt Beulah, the widow of their father's uncle, had offered to take all three of them. They'd been grateful for her actions, but they'd come to love and admire the woman, too.

She'd taught Abby, and the others, everything she knew about ranching, and it had been considerable. When she'd physically been unable to run the ranch, Abby had taken over, reporting to her each night about the events of the day.

Melissa, her middle sister, had been a natural housekeeper, remaining at home most of the time to cook and clean. Beth, her baby sister, had worked with her, an expert rider and hard worker.

When Aunt Beulah had died, the sisters had been startled to discover themselves millionaires. Their aunt had invested oil money when the boom was big in Texas and never touched it. They decided they should each pursue their dreams.

Beth wanted to follow the rodeo, barrel-racing, but she married her trainer and now was expecting a child. She and Jed Davis had moved to the farm across from the Circle K ranch, where he trained riders and horses for the rodeo circuit.

Melissa had wanted to take care of children who'd been orphaned as they had been. She built a house on the ranch and started taking in foster children. Now she, too, was married, to Abby's former manager and, counting Rob's daughter Terri, their family consisted of six children, two foster daughters and three children they'd adopted.

She, Rob and their adopted children had formed a new corporation recently, called ProRide, supplying rodeo stock. It had become immensely successful overnight and explained why she was having to interview for another manager for the cattle operation.

Since family was important to Abby, she appreciated the fact that Logan Crawford didn't want to abandon his. And she could understand why he wanted to get away, too.

"If you'd give me a chance, Miss Kennedy, I think I could show you I'd do a good job."

His deep voice rumbled through his chest and Abby felt the vibrations as she clasped his waist. She'd told him no interview, but he'd been ignoring those words, giving her information, trying to sway her opinion.

"I don't think it would work, Mr. Crawford."

It was awkward to reject someone when her arms

were around him. Thank goodness she didn't have
to face him.

"Why?"

"Because I'd be peering over your shoulder as
much as your brothers did." That was the best argument she had. And she thought it was an important one.

"Of course you would. It's your place. You'd
have the right."

His answer surprised her. She hadn't expected
him to be reasonable.

"But you said—"

"I said my brothers bothered me. I never objected
to my father's supervision. Or our foreman's. They
had the right. But Joe, Pete and Rick aren't that
much older than I am. We're all a year apart."

"Your poor mother," she muttered.

"Yeah, she reminds us of that frequently," he
said, and she could hear a smile in his voice.

"So, it seems to me I have as much right as the
others to run things. I certainly have as much knowledge."

His words gave her a lot to think about. His ap-
plication had been by far the best she'd received.
Was she making a hasty decision because she'd
been embarrassed that he'd discovered her fear of
snakes? That he'd seen her acting like a helpless
heroine from a century ago?

Before she could come to any decisions, she heard
the rumbling of hooves from horses moving quickly.
Then, over the hill, several riders appeared.

They pulled to an abrupt halt when they reached
Crawford's mount.

"Abby, you okay?" Floyd, one of her hands, demanded.

"Yes, Floyd. Did Ruby make it back to the barn?"

"Yeah. Ellen called us. She was worried. What happened?" Before she could answer, he nodded to her companion. "Thanks for helping Abby."

Since not only Floyd had come, but also Barney and he was leading a mount for her, Abby nudged the man in front of her. "If you'll move your foot, I'll get down."

He twisted his body as he moved his boot and offered his arm to help her dismount. With relief, she reached the ground and grabbed for the reins Barney held out to her. "Thanks," she told him as she swung into the saddle.

"By the way, guys, this is Logan Crawford. He's come to interview for the job as manager. This is Floyd and Barney, two of my hands."

She watched in approval as Logan Crawford offered a hand to each man, easily sitting his horse.

"You from around here?" Floyd asked.

"Couple of hours away. Oklahoma."

Barney nodded.

Floyd muttered, "I was working a spread in Oklahoma before I came here." He gave his former boss's name and stared at Logan.

The man laughed. "Didn't last long? A lot of men don't. Can't stomach his ways."

Abby watched in surprise as tension left Floyd's body. He grinned at the stranger.

Floyd had married her housekeeper, Ellen, a few

months ago, and felt a special protectiveness for Abby, though she'd told him it wasn't necessary.

But it appeared he was no longer suspicious about Logan Crawford.

"That wasn't where you worked?" Floyd asked.

"Not likely," he assured him with a grin. "I was on my dad's place, the Double C."

Floyd's eyes widened. "Nice spread."

"I heard of that place," Barney put in. "It's prime."

"Thanks."

"So why you wanting to come here?"

"It's time for me to spread my wings," Logan said.

Abby, able to see Logan's expression this time, noted that his explanation took a different form for the men, but it was basically the same reason.

Floyd turned to beam at her. "Hey, you got lucky, Abby, getting a Crawford from the Double C for a manager. Good thing Ellen made apple cobbler for dinner so's we can celebrate."

All three men stared at her, waiting for her to agree.

Chapter Two

Logan kept an easy smile on his face, hoping Abigail Kennedy's men would persuade her to give him a chance. But he, unlike Floyd and Barney, knew she wasn't convinced.

"I haven't made up my mind about the job," she muttered and swung her horse around with skill. "Call Ellen and tell her we're coming in so she won't worry," she ordered over her shoulder as she set her horse in motion.

Relieved that she hadn't given a definite no, Logan kept pace with Barney, leaving Floyd to ride beside the lady. He didn't want to press the issue right now.

"What's the setup, Barney? Why did the last manager quit?"

"Aw, he didn't really quit. They started a supply company for the rodeos. Abby's other brother-in-law, Jed Davis, has connections and it grew overnight. There's too much for Rob to be able to do everything. 'Specially with all them kids.''

"He has a big family?"

Barney chuckled. "I reckon. He married Abby's other sister, Melissa, and together they have six."

Logan's eyebrows rose. "Six! That's a lot. But somehow I got the impression from something Abby wrote that they'd only recently married."

"They're not natural kids. I mean, they got two foster girls. And then, right before they got married, three kids next door were orphaned. Melissa took them in and she and Rob adopted 'em. And there's his girl. So it's a crowd."

"I'd say. Though there were six kids at our house, too," he said with a smile, remembering some of the havoc they'd created for his poor mother.

Abby looked over her shoulder. "I thought you said you had four brothers."

It pleased him that she'd been listening to their conversation. Maybe he still had a chance. "I do, but I also have a baby sister."

"Why didn't you mention her?"

"Because she doesn't have anything to do with running the ranch," he told her, surprised by the question.

Abby reined in her horse and stared at him. "What does she do?"

"Do?" It was Logan's turn to be puzzled. "She helps Mom with the household when she's not in school."

"Oh, like Melissa did, doing the cooking and all?"

"Well, no, Lindsay doesn't actually cook. We

have a cook, or we'd all die of food poisoning," he said with a laugh. His sister had created a few notable disasters in the kitchen.

Abby was staring at him, not moving on, and he didn't know what else to say. Something was bothering her. He just didn't know what.

Floyd attempted to help. "I think Abby means what does she do with her time."

"What all women do. She socializes, shops, you know, girl things."

Abby turned and urged her horse forward. Which would make a man think he'd satisfied her curiosity, but he didn't think he had. And he wanted to know why.

Why did his sister's behavior affect his job?

When they reached the barn where his truck and trailer were parked, he didn't follow the men into the corral. His three other horses were still in the horse trailer, and he figured he'd better put Dusty in his place, too.

Abby turned to look at him.

"Bring your mount in here so you can rub him down, give him feed and water. You got other horses in the trailer?"

He nodded.

"You can unload them all. You'll spend the night, of course, no matter what happens."

He'd hoped for at least that much, but he wasn't about to presume. Miss Abigail Kennedy appeared to be a law unto herself.

"Thanks."

After he'd taken care of Dusty, he headed for his trailer and found Barney and Floyd beside him.

"We'll help," Barney assured him with a grin.

Abby stopped them. "Is Dirk still out in the south pasture?"

"Yes'm," Barney said. "He should be in soon." He squinted into the west. "Won't be light too much longer."

In late October, the sunlight didn't last all that long in north Texas.

"'Sides, Ellen said dinner would be ready at six," Floyd reminded her.

Logan grinned. Men who worked hard also ate hard. Seemed Floyd had food on his brain.

Abby nodded, but before she turned away, she added, "Would you take Mr. Crawford to the bunkhouse so he can clean up?"

"Sure. Want me to show him the manager's house?" Floyd asked.

Abby sighed, putting her hands on her hips.

Logan let his gaze rove over that part of her anatomy until he looked up and saw her glaring at him. Oops, not a good idea when he still didn't have the job. But hell, the woman was attractive.

"Yeah, fine," Abby muttered and started walking to the main house.

"I don't know what's got into Abby," Barney said in a soft voice. "She's usually more friendly. Hasn't been thrown from a horse in a long time, either. Not since she was a kid."

"There was a snake," Logan explained.

The ranch hands looked at each other, nodding.

"That explains it then. That little lady has one of them phobia things about snakes. She can't even stand the garden variety," Floyd said.

"She shouldn't have been out by herself," Logan commented, his gaze still fixed on Abby's feminine form.

When neither man responded, he looked back at them.

"Lordy, you don't want to be telling Abby that," Barney warned, though his grin indicated he wanted to be present if Logan committed that sin.

"Why not?"

"Abby's been riding by herself since she was twelve and first came here. Beulah didn't tolerate any sissiness."

"It's common sense, not sissiness," Logan assured him.

Both men ignored his assertion, opening the gate to his trailer.

The temptation to dress up for dinner upset Abby almost as much as the snake.

What had gotten into her? Logan Crawford was a cowboy, nothing more. She had no interest in any man. And she suspected, from what the man had said, that he'd have no interest in her.

"Girl things!" she snorted in disgust. "Shopping, socializing. Like we're good for nothing."

Well, Mr. Logan Crawford had some lessons to learn. And if it wouldn't be dangerous to keep him around, considering her response to him, she'd teach him.

But she'd realized when she put her arms around him, that touching him was a little too pleasurable. A little too distracting. It wouldn't do to hire him.

Now she had to convince Barney and Floyd that

she hadn't lost her mind. Floyd was already in Logan's corner. And since they needed more help, it wouldn't take much for Barney, and Dirk, too, to wonder what was wrong with her.

She was looking for another cowhand, but good ones were hard to come by. With Wayne, Melissa and Rob's adopted son and partner in ProRide with Abby and Rob, in school, his help was lost. He didn't have time after doing his homework. He'd been a real asset during the summer.

Rob had no time to give to the cattle operation, since he was running the mushrooming ProRide. So they needed more help.

She had an ad in several newspapers.

So far, no one had responded.

She dressed in a clean pair of jeans and deliberately added an old shirt, one that she'd considered adding to the rag pile just last week. Though she scrubbed her face, she didn't add any makeup.

No dolling up for Mr. Crawford.

As she reached the kitchen, the phone on the wall rang.

"I'll get it," she told Ellen, who was setting plates of food on the table.

Her sister Melissa spoke as soon as Abby answered. "Hi, I heard the new manager arrived."

Abby almost groaned aloud. "No. A man came to be interviewed, but—"

"Aren't you going to hire him?"

"I don't think so."

Silence followed. Then muffled words, as if Melissa had her hand over the receiver. "Uh, Abby? Rob wants to talk to you."

Her brother-in-law spoke next. "Hey, Abby, I thought I'd tell you if the man's from the Double C, like Melissa said, I've heard it's a good place."

"I know," Abby said with a sigh.

"Want me to come talk to him?"

Abby's spine stiffened, but she cautioned herself. After all, Rob had never treated her as less than anyone else because she was a woman. "I think I can handle it, thanks, Rob."

"Okay." He handed the phone back to Melissa.

"We thought we'd come have dessert with you, so we could welcome—meet the man. Ellen asked us. Is that a problem?"

What could she say? Yes, it's a problem. I don't want you to meet him because I'm going to get rid of him as soon as possible because he's—he's too attractive.

No, she couldn't say that. "Of course, you're welcome. Are the kids coming?"

Melissa laughed, a musical sound that always heartened Abby. Melissa was happy with her life. "No, we don't want to cause too much turmoil. I fixed something for them."

"Okay. We'll see you in a little while."

When she hung up the phone, she turned around to see Ellen staring at her, a look of apprehension on her face. "Sorry, Abby. He...I mean, I thought Logan seemed perfect. I just assumed..."

Ellen was wonderful, both with her cooking and her care of Abby and all her family. She couldn't hurt the lady's feelings. "Don't worry about it." Then she gave a resigned grin. "I suppose you invited Beth and Jed, too?"

Ellen nodded.

Abby blew out her breath. Damn. She was feeling trapped. "Well, we'll have a full house tonight. Is it your apple cobbler, like Floyd said?"

"Yes. I baked two, so we'd have plenty. And there's ice cream to go on top."

It would taste like acid to Abby.

The sound of boots on the back porch had her drawing a deep breath and bracing herself. Showtime.

Half an hour later, the meal was almost over. Abby hadn't managed to eat much. She'd spent most of the time avoiding Logan's glances.

He fit in well with the cowhands. Even though he was the son of a wealthy rancher, he didn't expect special treatment, a point in his favor. Nor did he act like a know-it-all. He didn't quibble about taking his plate to the sink, as Jed, Beth's husband, had initiated when he'd arrived.

A quick knock on the back door announced her family's arrival. Ellen hurried over, wiping her hands on her apron. "Come in, come in."

Abby remained silent and after a quick glance at her, Ellen made the introductions. After shaking hands with Logan, Jed and Rob pulled extra chairs up to the long table.

Beth was almost six months pregnant and Jed hovered over her constantly. She complained, but she always wore a contented smile, so Abby didn't take her complaints seriously. Now she sighed as she sank into a chair.

"You okay, hon?" Jed asked.

She gave him a sweet smile before winking at Abby. "Sure. Just a little tired."

"I told you to let Clara do the laundry," Jed complained, watching her like a hawk.

Melissa laughed. "Jed, she's pulling your leg."

"What?"

Abby gave Beth a stern look. "She's teasing you, Jed. Don't worry about her. She won't overdo it."

"Spoilsports," Beth said to her sisters. Then she put her elbows on the table and looked at Logan Crawford. "Do you have sisters, Mr. Crawford?"

"Yes, I have one sister. And she appears to be as spoiled as you, Mrs. Davis." He grinned at Beth, showing he meant no offense.

Abby didn't care. He had no business saying such a thing about her sister. Stiffly she said, "Beth's a hard worker."

She realized she'd overreacted when both her sisters looked at her in surprise. But she wouldn't apologize.

Fortunately, Jed Davis, Beth's husband, picked up the conversation. "Heard you're one of Caleb Crawford's sons. He's got a beauty of a place."

"Thanks. You've been there?"

"I stopped by to evaluate a horse for one of your brothers, Pete, I think it was. I didn't think the animal was worth the time it would've taken to train him."

"Yeah, I remember that. Last spring, wasn't it?" Logan asked, frowning.

"Yeah."

"Turned out you were right. We sold the horse, explaining what you'd said, but the man didn't take our word for it. Pete talked to him a couple of weeks ago. Things didn't work out.''

Jed nodded.

Abby wasn't surprised. She'd never met anyone as good with horses as Jed Davis. Which explained why his training center was so successful.

Rob asked a question about Logan's experience while Ellen started serving the cobbler and ice cream. Both Abby and Melissa got up to help her, but they both motioned for Beth to stay seated.

After Dirk and Barney had finished their dessert, they excused themselves. Then Floyd and Ellen retired to their attached apartment. Abby had had it added on to the house after their marriage. It gave them more privacy than one of the bedrooms upstairs.

Which now left Abby the entire top floor to herself.

Sometimes, it got a little lonesome.

"What do you think, Abby?" Rob asked.

She looked up in surprise. "I'm sorry, I didn't hear the question."

"You shouldn't bother her with that stuff," Logan said, smiling easily. "I'm sure she wouldn't have an opinion anyway."

Both Rob and Jed stared at Logan.

"What stuff would that be, Mr. Crawford?" Abby demanded, her voice tight.

"I was talking about wheat futures, Miss Kennedy, and the advisability of buying extra wheat for this winter." He said it almost apologetically, as if he didn't want to worry her pretty little head.

Abby ground her teeth. Then she took a sip of

iced tea. When she felt perfectly in control, she said, "We've purchased twenty percent more hay this year, even though we had a bumper crop ourselves. The predictions for winter are for a long one, and the prices are below the market norm at the moment. I decided it was a good risk."

He raised one eyebrow, his grin still in place, as he asked, "Do you have good storage so it won't go bad?"

She couldn't keep herself from taunting him a little. "You mean you have to store hay? I thought you just piled it up in the pasture so the little old cows could eat whenever they wanted."

He didn't lose his grin as the others laughed. "Sorry. I guess that was a dumb question." He paused, then added, "Barney told me how much land you've got here. Seems to me you'd need more help."

This time her voice was crisp, businesslike. "I'm advertising for another hand."

"How do you manage?"

As if he realized she didn't like that question more than the others, Rob cleared his throat and hurriedly answered. "We were only half that size when I came here. But when our neighbors were killed, Melissa and I adopted the kids and we're running both operations as one. Then we added the rodeo supply company and, well, things just multiplied."

"Business is good?"

Rob chuckled. "Good? Thanks to Jed, here, who has all the rodeo connections, it's better than good."

"So, my responsibilities would be the cattle operation?"

Again, Rob answered. "Theoretically, yeah. But you know how it is on a ranch. We all put our backs to whatever needs to be done. It'll be roundup next week, and I'll be helping with that."

Abby decided it was time she entered the conversation again. "Did you handle any of the breeding on the Double C?"

He gave her cautious look she didn't understand. "Some."

"We've been using the sperm of Red Dog. Have you had any of his babies?" She didn't own that bull, but they had bought the sperm and had the cows artificially inseminated last year. The crop had been outstanding.

He looked at Rob. "We used him some. But we found we had more success with Scalawag from the King Ranch. Have you tried him?"

Rob looked at her.

Abby glared at their guest. Did he think he could ignore her? "No, we haven't. What were the advantages?"

Logan rubbed his chin, then looked directly at Abby. "Frankly, Miss Kennedy, I'm not used to discussing breeding at the dinner table. My mother didn't allow that kind of conversation in her presence."

Abby had suspected as much. "Then it's fortunate you're returning to your mother's table, where you'll be comfortable, isn't it?" She shoved back her chair. "If you'll excuse me, everyone, I have some paperwork to do. I'll leave a check with Ellen for your trouble, Mr. Crawford."

And she walked out of the kitchen.

* * *

"Whew!" Rob said, leaning back in his chair. "You like to do things the hard way, don't you?"

"What did I do?" Logan asked, a puzzled look on his face. "I mean, obviously I upset her, but I was only trying to be polite."

Melissa leaned toward him, a gentle smile on her face. "Abby is no neophyte, Mr. Crawford. She's spent seventeen years learning ranching from our aunt Beulah. She drags in after long hours in the saddle and does the paperwork. Then she reads all the journals. She even took some correspondence courses from Texas A & M."

Logan studied her. "Okay. I can appreciate that she has a certain knowledge, but—"

Beth laughed. "Melissa, you're being too polite. Mr. Crawford, you don't have a snowball's chance in hell of working for Abby if you don't respect her abilities."

"I didn't say I don't respect—"

"Yes, you did. You tried to talk to Rob, even when Abby asked the question. And you made her feel crass with your remarks about your mother's standards of behavior." She drew a deep breath, before she added, "And if you think any of us will encourage her to hire you, you've got marbles in your brain. No one attacks Abby around here."

Jed put his arm around his wife. "Calm down, sweetheart. He didn't mean to. I don't think he's been around a woman like Abby before."

"Look," Logan began, his cheeks red, "I didn't mean to…I thought she might be…it's a little awkward to discuss breeding with a woman."

Melissa said, "You were supposed to discuss breeding with a rancher, Mr. Crawford. Abby is a rancher. The fact that she's also a woman is incidental."

Logan looked at the two men, hoping for some support. They both grinned at him, clearly aware of his dilemma, but they didn't explain to their wives.

Much to his relief, Jed finally said, "Mind if we walk Logan down to the barn? I want to see his mounts."

Logan practically leaped to his feet, eager to escape the feminine censure on the ladies' faces.

"I'll be glad to show you. I'm particularly proud of a couple of them that I raised and trained."

Both men kissed their wives, then stood and led the way out of the house.

Logan nodded to both women, muttered the word sorry and hurried after the two men, realizing they were his only hope.

Chapter Three

Logan said nothing until the three men reached the safety of the barn. When they did, he didn't bother with subtlety. "Have I completely blown it?"

Jed and Rob looked at each other.

Finally Rob shrugged his shoulders. "Probably. Abby's a little sensitive about this female thing."

"Hell, I can't treat her like a man when she looks like—I mean, she's a damn beautiful woman. And she wanted me to sit at the table and talk about breeding?" By the time he finished, he was shouting.

In the deafening silence, the other two men burst into laughter.

"Is this a practical joke?" Logan asked, bewildered. He was used to teasing. Hell, with four brothers, he wouldn't have survived if he wasn't. That was the only explanation for their hilarity.

"No, man, no joke. Abby was dead serious," Jed assured him, still grinning.

"Then what's so funny?"

Rob attempted to wipe the grin from his face, but remnants remained when he took his hand down. "I think that was sympathy breaking out."

"You had problems with Abby?"

"No, no," Rob said hurriedly, "but we—each of us had trouble with another lady."

Logan actually took several steps backward before he caught himself. "Oh, no! I know what you mean. You're talking about your wives, aren't you?"

"Yeah," Jed agreed, still smiling.

"Look, I'm not—that's not what it is. I don't have time to take care of a woman right now."

Rob jostled Jed with his elbow and said soothingly, "Of course not. Now, what are you going to do about Abby? Are you still interested in the job?"

Logan frowned. His immediate instinct was to assure the two men he still wanted the job. But he wasn't sure why. It was perfectly located for his purposes, of course. And the facilities were good. He liked the men. It would be a privilege to work with these two. But— "I guess so."

"Well, we'll talk to her. But I don't know if we'll be able to convince her. She can be hardheaded." He grinned again. "It runs in the family."

"Yeah," Jed agreed wholeheartedly.

"So, you think I should try again in the morning?"

"Sure, but don't say anything like you did tonight. Think of Abby as a man," Rob cautioned.

Logan opened his mouth to protest. Damn it, the man was asking the impossible. Then he gave an abrupt nod.

"Good," Jed said, clapping him on the back, as if they'd shared hard times. "You'll do fine."

"You got a bed in the bunkhouse?" Rob asked.

"Yeah, Floyd and Barney showed me where to sleep."

"Well, breakfast comes early. I hope you're at your best in the morning," Jed said with another smile before he and Rob headed back to the house.

Logan stood there, comfortable in the barn, used to the familiar sounds, feeling unsettled. This had been a crazy day. From the moment he'd met Abby Kennedy.

And tomorrow didn't look much better.

Abby hadn't gotten much work done. Over and over she replayed the scene at the table. And got angry each time. She wouldn't be treated like a—a fluttery Southern belle.

Aunt Beulah wouldn't have stood for it!

Didn't matter that the woman was dead. She'd left Abby a heritage more important than the ranch. She'd left her self-esteem, determination, independence.

Sometimes Abby wished she was more like her sisters. Each had met the love of her life and been able to marry and be happy. Beth was having a baby. Melissa had six children to surround her with love.

Abby had cows.

But she could take care of herself…and her cows.

She could keep the ranch running at a profit. Provide jobs for good men. And be a great aunt.

And she wasn't going to let any man tell her to sit on a shelf and look pretty!

A rueful chuckle broke through her anger. A good thing, since looking pretty might be nigh to impossible. Beth and Melissa had gotten all the pretty genes. Her hair didn't curl like Beth's. Her eyes weren't green like Melissa's, just a plain blue. She was taller than both of them and didn't have quite as many curves.

Oh, she was definitely female. No one had ever mistaken her for a man, but she wasn't date bait. There'd only been one date in high school. She'd been working too hard on the ranch to worry about it, but—

Aunt Beulah had encouraged her to take a few classes at the junior college in Wichita Falls until they'd gotten shorthanded. There Abby had met Daniel Wicks. He was a handsome man. Inexperienced, blinded by hormones, Abby had thought she was in love.

Then he'd told her, after she'd refused to sleep with him, that she wasn't feminine enough for him. He liked pretty girls.

She'd cried on Aunt Beulah's shoulder. The woman had told her to be strong. To take care of business. To ignore men.

So here was another handsome face trying to point out that she wasn't feminine enough.

A knock on the door brought her out of her thoughts.

"Come in."

Her two brothers-in-law walked into her office. "Hi, guys. I thought you would've gone home by now. I know Beth needs her rest."

She expected Jed to rush right out and see to his wife. Instead he stayed planted in her doorway.

"Thought we'd mention we talked to Crawford," Rob said, a smile on his face. "He's a good man, knowledgeable."

Abby said nothing.

"Course, he has one little problem," Jed added.

"Only one?" Abby asked.

"He's not used to working with women, I think," Jed said. "You could teach him a lot, and he'd be good for the ranch, but I can understand if you're not up to the challenge."

Abby rolled her eyes. "The few classes I took at junior college included Psychology 101, Jed. Nice try."

"Good men are hard to find," Rob said.

"So I've heard," Abby drawled.

"Roundup is next week, and I'm not going to be able to help out much," Jed reminded her.

"Save your breath," Abby said before Rob could come up with another reason to hire Logan Crawford. "I'm not hiring him, so give it up."

"You're the boss, Abby. A fact that hasn't escaped Logan, either," Rob said. "You could give him another chance."

Abby gave a big sigh. "Good night, dear brothers. Tell my sisters good night for me."

"You're a hardhearted woman, Abby Kennedy," Jed told her, but his grin took the sting out of his words.

Both men waved their goodbyes and closed the door behind them.

Abby bowed her head into her hands. What a day. And though Scarlett O'Hara's words were meant to be optimistic, she could only think tomorrow would be another day...just like this one. Oh, dear!

Abby considered remaining in her bedroom the next morning until she saw Logan Crawford drive away.

But that would be cowardly, and Aunt Beulah had taught her better. So she plaited her long hair, as usual, donned her normal gear of jeans, a shirt, and boots, then ran down the stairs. Ellen was putting breakfast on the table and Floyd had just gone outside to ring the dinner bell on the back porch.

"Mornin'," Abby said. Her first action was to grab the mug by her plate and fill it with hot, black coffee. After a long sip, she muttered, "Mmm, I needed that."

Floyd, having come back in, asked, "Didn't you sleep good?"

"So-so."

"I would'a thought you'd sleep like a baby now that you got some good help." He was beaming at her.

She'd forgotten that Ellen and Floyd had gone to bed before the debacle last evening. "Uh, Floyd, I'm not hiring Crawford."

"What? But Abby——"

"He won't work for a woman." That was a loose interpretation of the facts, but Abby felt justified. If the man couldn't discuss all aspects of ranching with her, she didn't see how they could work together.

Floyd frowned. "He didn't seem like that kind of a man."

The back door opened and Dirk and Barney, followed by Logan, entered the kitchen. Abby greeted everyone at once and avoided looking at the handsome cowboy. As she sat down at the head of the table, Floyd picked up the coffeepot and began filling everyone's cup.

"Breakfast smells good, Ellen. You sure feed everyone well," Logan said, a smile on his face.

Since she'd been watching him out of the corner of her eye, Abby figured he wasn't disturbed about not getting the job. Not with that smile on his face.

Much to her surprise, breakfast seemed almost normal. Barney and Dirk seldom ever talked. Floyd usually kept up a stream of conversation, but not today. Logan made occasional comments, but nothing about his situation or ranching in general.

She supposed he was following his mother's edicts. Fine. It helped her avoid any awkwardness.

When she finished eating, she was prepared to fetch the check she'd written the night before from her office and hand it over to Crawford. Then she would be rid of the man.

She'd have to start the process all over again to hire a manager. Since his was the only decent résumé she'd received, she couldn't even fall back on those she had on file.

"Mr. Crawford," she began as she stood, only to be interrupted by the phone. "I'll get it."

"Miss Abby, we got problems," said Duffy, the

old man who was general caretaker on the Prine ranch, Melissa and Rob's adopted children's acreage.

"What is it, Duffy?"

"The fence between here and Pritchard's place is down and that prime herd you had in the east pasture is mixing with his cows."

"Okay, a couple of us will be right over," she said, frowning, trying to juggle her workforce.

"You'd better hurry. That no-account bull is in there and you're going to have some sorry babies if he gets with any of your heifers."

"Damn!" She'd scheduled that herd for artificial insemination for tomorrow morning, just before roundup. Her neighbor's bull wasn't acceptable. "Okay, do what you can. We'll put on some speed."

"What's up?" Floyd asked at once, and she turned to discover all eyes on her.

She gave a brief synopsis of the situation. The problem was she already had a herd that needed moving in preparation for next week. She'd intended to send all three men to move it closer in.

"Dirk and Barney, do you think you can move that herd by yourselves? Floyd and I will go help Duffy. Floyd, I need you to hitch up the horse trailer."

"Don't you remember, Abby? It got a flat tire two days ago. I haven't had a chance to deal with it," Floyd returned, looking as worried as Abby felt.

"If you could use some extra help, I'll be glad to pitch in," Logan said quietly. "My rig is ready to go."

"No, I can't—"

Floyd interrupted her. "Don't let pride get in your way, Abby girl."

She glared at him, then turned back to Logan. "It would be unfair to take advantage of you."

To her surprise, he grinned. "Yeah. But if we made it a bet, it wouldn't."

"What kind of bet?"

"If I perform up to your expectations today, you give me the job on a trial basis, one month. If you don't like what you see, I'm out of here this afternoon, with everything even between us."

She hesitated. The bet was stacked in her favor since her opinion was the determining factor. And she could use him…and his trailer. Finally she stuck out her hand. "You've got a deal, Mr. Crawford. Thanks."

Now it was his turn to hesitate. After staring at her hand, he finally took it and gave a brief shake. "Deal." Then he turned to Floyd. "Let's go load up. You know which horse Abby will want?"

"Sure do. She'll want Ruby. She's her favorite."

"Unless there are any snakes," Logan teased, cutting a grin at Abby even as he hurried from the kitchen.

Abby stood there openmouthed. Then she muttered, "I thought I was the boss."

Barney, getting up from the table, said, "Wasn't that what you wanted? For them to load up?"

That wasn't the point. Or maybe it was. Was she afraid to hire Logan Crawford because he might make her appear as useless as he considered women to be? Was she fearful he knew more than she did? Was she that small of a person?

By the time she reassured herself, Barney and Dirk had said their goodbyes and left the kitchen, and Ellen was clearing the table.

"I'll fix some lunch and bring it over to you."

"Okay, thanks, Ellen. We'll be over on the east side of the Prine place." Then she hurried up the stairs for her leather gloves, chaps and hat. She even added a lightweight jacket. October could turn chilly in a moment's notice.

When she reached the barn, Floyd and Logan were ready and waiting. She didn't want to admit to enjoying the fact that she hadn't had to do any of the loading. But she did.

Floyd held open the passenger side door of the truck and gestured for her to slide in just as Logan got behind the wheel. She didn't want to sit between the two men. She didn't want to sit close to Logan Crawford.

But if she put up a fuss, Floyd would wonder what was going on.

Floyd gave directions as Logan drove quickly and efficiently. Abby sat silently.

"What happened to the fences?" he finally asked.

"I don't know. I thought they were all in good shape. Didn't you and Dirk check them last month?" Abby asked Floyd.

"We did. They were good enough to hold together. I don't know what happened."

"You did pack fencing material so we can make repairs, didn't you?"

"Yup. Logan reminded me."

Abby forced herself to mutter, "Thanks." She should've reminded Floyd before he went to the barn, but she'd been too flustered by Logan's offer. She couldn't keep the man around because she was less than she should be when he distracted her.

"I'm sure Floyd would've thought of it. How big a herd are we talking about?"

"A little over two hundred."

"We've got our work cut out for us. Maybe if we tie up the bull first, there won't be too many repercussions."

"If Pritchard will let us. He loves that ornery critter. He'll probably want to charge me if his bull impregnates any of my cows," Abby grumbled.

Both men laughed and Floyd added, "You got that right."

When they reached the place of the breakthrough, Abby discovered a long length of fence down. And it looked to her as if it had been cut.

The sharp look Logan sent her told her he thought so, too, but she briefly shook her head. She'd deal with whatever was going on after she'd retrieved her herd.

After the horses were unloaded, the three of them mounted and rode onto Pritchard's land. Abby assumed the owner was aware of the problem.

It only took a couple of minutes to find the herd over the next hill. Duffy was in conversation with Pritchard, Abby realized at once. And they were the only ones there. Pritchard hadn't brought any hands to help out.

"Damn!" she muttered under her breath.

"We haven't drawn a crowd, have we?" Logan said softly.

"No." Abby's clipped tone was due to the anger building in her, not Logan's comment. "We have the Circle K brand on the right hip. Pritchard tags his in the ear."

"Right." Without any more words, Logan, with Floyd following him, began separating the cows, pushing those with her brand toward the broken fence.

She rode over to her neighbor and Duffy.

"Morning. What happened?"

Duffy shrugged but Abby saw awareness in his eyes.

Cecil Pritchard said, "Looks like you didn't tend your fences like you should've. I told you you were taking on too much. That place should be sold so it can be productive." Pritchard looked quite pleased with his words.

Abby suspected the man wanted the place himself. But she hadn't believed he'd pull something like this. "We'll clear our cows out as soon as possible. Where's your bull?"

The man looked downright gleeful at her question. "You hopin' for some free babies? He's here, out there enjoying himself. You might get lucky."

Abby tried to contain the urge to wipe that smirk off his face. "I'm not interested in bad luck." Then she turned to the man beside her. "Let's get to work, Duffy."

She didn't expect any help from her neighbor, and she got none. But Logan and Floyd had already made inroads. The first thing Logan had done, Floyd told her later, was rope the bull and tie him to a tree.

Then the hard work began.

Abby worked as hard as the others. Ruby had been well-trained. But she also kept an eye on her men. Before too long, Logan had suggested Duffy guard the fence break, keeping the ones they'd sorted out on the right side of it.

He'd made the right choice. Duffy was older and not as agile as he'd once been. By the time Ellen came with lunch, there were only a few cows remaining. And Pritchard, after protesting the treatment of his bull, had retreated.

Abby could thank Logan for that, too. Pritchard had apparently figured a woman and two older men wouldn't put up much of a fuss. Logan was the one he ran into first.

Abby started in their direction, knowing the man intended to create more problems. Before she got there, he'd turned tail and disappeared.

"What did he say?"

Logan paused and grinned at her. "He wanted to make sure I was gentle with his baby."

She wasn't sure she believed him. "That's all?"

"He mentioned he'd like the bull turned loose."

She waited, not bothering to ask.

"I told him I'd take care of that personally." With a wink, he added, "I just didn't say when."

Abby looked at her watch. "He'll be back."

"I figured. He got it in for you?"

She knew what he was asking. Why had the fence been cut? With a sigh, she said, "I think he hoped to buy the land after the Prines' death."

Logan nodded, as if that was what he suspected. "Ellen's here with some food."

"I think we can be finished in a couple of hours," he said, frowning.

"I know, but we've all worked hard. We'll grab a bite to eat and work better." She waited for him to argue with her. She suspected he liked to do things his way. To her surprise, he nodded and turned his horse toward the break in the fence.

With a relieved sigh, Abby followed him. He'd made a difference today. A big difference. They wouldn't be nearly as far along without him. He'd secured Pritchard's bull to keep him from doing any more harm. And he'd handled her neighbor without making the situation worse.

She appreciated what he'd done.

Until she realized that meant she'd have to hire him.

Damn!

Chapter Four

Logan certainly had no complaints about the way Abby fed her men. Ellen had provided thick roast beef sandwiches. In fact, the food could be considered a plus. Though he thought long and hard, he couldn't come up with any complaints at all.

About the running of the ranch.

He had a few concerns about Abby Kennedy. For one, she was distracting. His gaze remained fastened on her backside and long legs as she swung out of the saddle. Fantasies of those legs wrapped around him, her curves pressed against him, almost caused him to step in a cowpie as he dismounted.

Then there was her work. Not that he could complain about it. She never let up, pushing herself more than anyone. Ruby, her cow pony, was well-trained, and Abby sat the saddle with ease.

His mother and sister both rode well, but they never worked on the ranch. His mother had always said women were too delicate to handle such things. She preferred maintaining the family's place in the county. She served on the hospital board, the school board, the charity committee. Teas were her strength.

Logan didn't know how to respond to a beautiful woman who could do a man's job.

"Logan?" Ellen called. "Here's a soda to go with your sandwich."

"Thanks, Ellen. These are great sandwiches."

Floyd, always a champion of his wife's skills, said, "Wait until tonight. She's frying chicken. It's the best."

Logan grinned. Floyd he understood.

"I'll send Floyd over with some for you, Duffy," Ellen said to the older man.

He had to be over sixty. He'd worked hard today, but Logan could tell he didn't have much left in him. "Good job this morning, Duffy. Floyd and I couldn't have managed without you."

There was a sudden silence and he looked up to discover Abby glaring at him. "I mean, Floyd, Abby and I couldn't have managed without you." He hadn't meant to minimize Abby's contribution. He just wasn't used to including a woman. "Who trained Ruby, Abby? She's a fine cutter."

"I did," she said crisply. Then she reluctantly added, "With Barney's help."

Nothing more was said as they all ate, sitting on the back of the two trucks. When they finished, he stepped closer to Abby. She should smell like horse, sweat and cows. And she did. But there was an elusive flower scent that made those smells blend into an elixir.

"Uh, I think we can manage without Duffy now, if there's something else he can be doing. Maybe something a little less energetic?"

Her gaze cut to the old man and she gave a brief nod. Then she moved to Duffy's side. "I think we've got things under control here, Duffy. I'd really appreciate it if you'd check all the fences that we share with Pritchard. I don't want another incident like today's."

"You sure, Abby? I can manage if you need me."

"I know, and I appreciate the offer, but I need the assurance that the fences have been checked." She gave the old man her best smile.

"You got it. I'll go north first. I don't think there's a herd in the south pasture."

"Good."

"Here, Duffy, take some cookies and an apple with you," Ellen said, stepping forward.

"Don't mind if I do."

He mounted and headed along the fence in a northerly direction.

As if following unspoken orders, the others turned to their mounts.

"Uh, Abby, why don't you go on back with Ellen? Floyd and I can manage," Logan suggested.

She turned her head sharply to stare at him. "I don't need to be put out to pasture, Crawford. I'll go when the job's done and not before."

He'd blown it again, he knew. But he'd been raised to spare women any hard labor. And the men could manage without her. It would just take a little longer. Shrugging his shoulders, he swung into the saddle.

Floyd rode up next to him. "Watch that or you'll be out on your ear," he whispered.

He figured Floyd was right. But, damn it, she'd worked like a Trojan all morning. She deserved a break.

A couple of hours later, the Circle K cows were on the right side of the fence. Logan left Floyd to start unloading the fencing materials while he released Pritchard's bull.

And none too soon.

Pritchard came riding over the hill, accompanied by several cowhands.

"Ain't you untied him yet? He's probably suffering!" the man growled at Logan.

"From frustration?" Logan asked, raising one brow. Did the man think he was stupid?

"If there's any damage done, I'll sue," the man threatened.

"Sue away," Logan muttered. He couldn't stand the blowhard. He loosened the rope around the bull's neck and deftly maneuvered his horse away from the horns. Though the bull lunged toward him, he and his horse moved quickly to the fence line where Floyd and Abby were working.

"Abby, why don't you take Dusty and keep an eye on that bull until we get the fence finished?" he suggested. While he didn't think the bull would be so angry he'd expend enough energy to charge them, he'd prefer some kind of defense.

And as strong as Abby appeared to be, she wasn't

as strong as him, which meant he could handle the fencing better.

She narrowed her blue eyes, as if accusing him of something, but Floyd spoke up.

"Yeah, Abby. We can get it done faster with Logan's muscles, and I don't like the look of that bull."

"I'll ride Ruby," she said, glowering at Logan.

He shrugged again. "Suit yourself, but Dusty's bigger and has worked around bulls. I'd hate for Ruby to be hurt."

While she struggled to decide, he swung down from the saddle and handed her his reins. She reluctantly took them. "He doesn't mind another rider?"

"No. He's well-trained."

The sound of pounding hooves had them all spinning around. But it wasn't the bull charging. Pritchard and his two cowboys were riding down on them.

Abby swung into the saddle, but she remained by her two men. Pritchard didn't rein his horse in until the last minute, scattering dirt and grass in their direction.

Logan admired the way Abby held her ground, keeping her posture casual. Her neighbor deserved a punch in the nose.

"I want to look at your cattle." Pritchard's words were a demand, not a request.

"Any particular reason?" Abby asked, her voice mild.

"Want to make sure you didn't take some of my prime heifers."

Floyd gasped, and Abby's features appeared to have been set in stone. Logan knew the man's words were tantamount to accusing Abby of cattle rustling. He stepped to Dusty's head, grabbing the reins.

Instead of letting her temper flare, Abby stared at her neighbor. Then she said, "Feel free. It will probably take about half an hour to fix the fence. You've got that long."

The man appeared taken aback by Abby's agreeable response. It seemed to Logan that his intent had been to upset Abby, not look for cattle.

Pritchard motioned to his men to cross over onto the Prine land. The two men looked embarrassed but they followed their boss's orders.

Abby never moved, continuing to stare at Pritchard. Logan wasn't sure who'd win the staring contest, but he motioned to Floyd to help him and they began to repair the fence.

After a couple of minutes, Pritchard left the fence line and went to examine his bull.

"I hope you didn't disturb a hair on that miserable, mangy bull," Abby muttered just loud enough for Logan and Floyd to hear. "If you did, he'll sue me for sure."

Logan kept his head down, using pliars to twist the new wire to the standing post. "A jury of peers would dismiss it if it ever got that far. You have nothing to worry about."

"I know. But it would be unpleasant," she added with a sigh.

Those words brought Logan's gaze to her. "From what I can tell, you'd handle it just fine. Just like you did now."

She seemed surprised by his approval. He offered her a smile, then hurriedly turned back to the fencing, before he forgot where he was and pulled her off the horse into his arms.

That thought made his face heat up. Damn it, she was his boss, at least for today. What was wrong with him? He'd never had this problem before. He almost laughed aloud at that thought. His dad and the manager of his dad's ranch never tempted him to distraction.

But he'd never worked for a woman. A beautiful woman. But even more tempting was a beautiful, courageous woman. The bully next door had intended to intimidate her, but she'd faced him down and turned the tables on him. He hadn't wanted to spend time looking at the cows they'd driven back onto the Prine ranch.

Pritchard's two hands came riding up just as they were ready to attach the last piece of fence.

"Just in time, boys," Logan called out. "We sure wouldn't want our handiwork to be cut...again." He gave them a hard stare.

"We don't want to cause no trouble," the older one mumbled.

"Good. Neither do we...unless we're provoked," Logan added, his voice loud, intended to carry the few feet to where Pritchard sat on his horse.

The men rode through the opening, then hurried to their boss's side. After a brief question, to which they responded by shaking their heads, Pritchard pulled his horse around in the direction of his house.

Before he rode off, however, he called, "You

keep those fences well tended. I don't want any
more botheration.''

Abby stared at him, a stubborn look on her face,
and said nothing. Logan and Floyd moved to stand
beside Dusty's head, letting the man know they were
aligned with their boss.

After the three horsemen disappeared, Logan said
to Abby, ''You'd better ride Dusty on through so
we can close up.''

Without speaking, she did as he requested, then
swung down from the saddle. As the men finished
up the fence, she led Dusty to the trailer behind Logan's truck and put him inside. Then she gathered
the reins for the other two horses and loaded them,
too.

Floyd and Logan threw the extra fencing and their
tools into the back of the truck and they all three
got inside.

''Whew,'' Floyd said, pulling a bandanna out of
his pocket and wiping his forehead. ''Thought we
might have a fight on our hands for a minute there.''

Logan cleared his throat. ''If Abby hadn't handled
things so well, we might have. Nice job, Abby.''

''Thanks. It's one of those times when it pays not
to have testosterone.''

Floyd laughed, and Logan smiled in agreement.
''Yeah. But I'd guess that's not the end of your
problems with that man. He's got a burr under his
saddle.''

Abby nodded but said nothing.

''Any idea why? It seems to be more than just
sour grapes over losing the land,'' Logan finally
asked. His father had always emphasized how im-

portant it was to have good relations with his neighbors.

Again Abby said nothing.

"Maybe you should ask the oldest boy," Floyd said, rubbing his chin. "Might be his daddy had problems with Pritchard before he died."

"That's a good idea, Floyd," Abby agreed, but she didn't speak to Logan.

He drove back to the ranch in silence. It was pretty obvious that he'd lost his gamble. The lady wanted nothing to do with him even after his hard work. If she wouldn't even speak to him, she sure wasn't going to keep him on as manager.

When he pulled the truck and trailer to a halt in front of the barn, Floyd was the first to speak. "Want me to go see how Dirk and Barney are doing? They maybe could use a little help."

"Would you mind, Floyd?" Abby asked, turning to look at him. "You're not too tired?"

"Naw, not me. And we got a couple of hours before dinnertime."

"Thanks. I'd come, too, but the kids will be home from school in a few minutes. I want to talk to Wayne. Then I'm going to call on the sheriff."

Logan frowned at her. "You going to report the wires being cut? You don't have any proof."

He hadn't meant to criticize her decision. He just wondered what it would accomplish. But she stiffened beside him.

"I know that. But Aunt Beulah—my aunt always believed in laying the groundwork. As you said, I don't think that will be the last problem I'll have with Pritchard. I want the sheriff up to speed if something else happens.''

''Good thinking,'' he agreed, nodding.

She seemed surprised again by his approval, but he said nothing else.

Floyd unloaded his horse. ''Want me to take care of Ruby, too, Abby? I'm going to change mounts before I head out.''

''No, let me take care of yours. You go ahead and check on the other guys.''

''Right,'' Floyd agreed and strode toward the barn.

Logan stood aside, waiting. Then he brought Dusty out of the trailer. After unsaddling the horse, he put the saddle in the trailer and led him to the corral where Abby was already taking care of Ruby.

''If you don't mind, I'll rub Dusty down before I load up,'' he said, watching her. He knew he was forcing the issue, but he wanted to hear her decision, even though he figured he already knew what it would be.

''You changed your mind about the job?'' she asked. Her gaze came up and met him over Ruby's back.

''No, but I figured you hadn't changed yours, either.''

She nibbled on her bottom lip and lust sucker punched him in his gut. That soft bottom lip had no lipstick on it to tempt a man, but he wanted to taste it, her, more than he'd ever wanted to taste a woman.

This was crazy. If he had any sense, he'd be

packed and headed down that road faster than he could say Jack Rabbit.

"I made a deal with you, Mr. Crawford. You kept your part of the bargain. The job is yours if you want it...for a month."

He stared at her. Then she ducked under Ruby's neck and came toward him, her hand extended. When her brows rose in question, he forced himself to take her hand. There was no softness in her fingers. They were strong, working hands. No delicate manicure, no creamy soft skin, protected from work.

She tugged against his hold, and he reluctantly released her. "I appreciate it, Abby. I'll try not to disappoint you."

"We'll talk again at the end of the month."

She turned back to the other horses, as if everything that needed to be said had been covered.

After her slim figure disappeared behind Ruby, he thought about what she'd said. "We'll talk before then, won't we? I mean, I'll need some direction about how you want things done."

"Of course. I meant we'd talk about you keeping the job. You may be fed up with us by then."

It struck him how reluctant he was to leave the Circle K after only being there two days. How would he feel after an entire month?

"Not the way Ellen cooks," he said lightly, hoping she wouldn't notice how her words had affected him.

Abby smiled, more relaxed than she'd been all day. "She is good, isn't she? Be grateful you're not dependent on me for meals. Melissa got all the cooking genes in our family.''

"We all have different talents," he assured her with a shrug. He'd seen a few of Abby's today and been impressed.

They continued to work on the horses in silence, but he watched his new boss out of the corner of his eye. When she started toward the house, he stopped her.

"Is there something in particular you want me to do until the others come in?''

"No. You can look at the manager's house, if you want. It's not locked. It should be in halfway decent shape. Rob lived there until last summer."

"How about I come with you to talk to the sheriff and the Prine boy?''

His suggestion seemed to surprise her. "Why would you do that?''

"I'd like to meet the kids who live on the ranch. And I'd be a second witness to the wire being cut for the sheriff.''

She frowned. "I don't guess I mind." Then she looked at him fiercely. "But I don't need you to baby-sit me. I can manage on my own.''

"I never doubted it for a minute, boss," he drawled. She strode past him, her nose in the air. He followed her, muttering under his breath, "As long as there are no snakes in sight.''

She heard his words. Her hands clenched into fists and her cheeks flamed. He was never going to let her forget her humiliation. But no matter. She'd made a deal and she was going to stick to it. Aunt Beulah taught her keeping her word was important.

For a month.

Inhaling a deep breath, she walked faster, hoping to put a little distance between the two of them, but Logan stayed only a step or two behind.

When they reached Melissa's front porch, Abby rapped on the door. She smiled when she heard the patter of little feet. Susie, the oldest of three little girls, pulled the door open. Then she announced over her shoulder, "It's Aunt Abby."

Abby knelt and hugged all three little girls. The two younger ones, Jessica and Mary Ann, were Melissa and Rob's foster daughters. They'd been abandoned, and without their parents signing a release, the two girls couldn't be adopted. Susie was the youngest Prine child and the formal adoption was almost completed for her and her two brothers.

Melissa came through the doorway from the kitchen. "Abby, come on...why, Logan, I didn't know...I mean, come on in, both of you. We're making cookies in the kitchen. Why don't you join us and sample our efforts?"

Suddenly, compared to the warm, maternal picture Melissa made, Abby felt grubby and ill-kempt. "We're kind of dirty, Melissa. I just—"

"Logan can use the bath down here, and Susie will show you to the one upstairs, Abby. Come down when you're ready."

Melissa ushered the two younger girls ahead of her into the kitchen, assuming they'd follow her directions.

"Meet you in the kitchen," Logan said with a grin, and walked off down the hall.

"Come on, Aunt Abby. The cookies are almost ready to come out of the oven."

"Tell you what, Susie, I know where the bathroom is. Why don't you go help Melissa, and I'll be there in a minute."

The child readily agreed and skipped off to the kitchen.

Abby hurried up the stairs, but what she really wanted to do was go hide in her own bedroom. Logan already thought she wasn't feminine. When he saw her next to Melissa, she was going to feel like the creature from the Black Lagoon.

She thought she was exaggerating until she faced herself in the bathroom mirror. A streak of dirt ran down one cheek, and wisps of hair had pulled lose from her braid, lying on her face and neck, damp with sweat.

Groaning, she began undoing the braid. Borrowing a nearby hairbrush, she brushed her hair and quickly rebraided it. Then she scrubbed her face, wishing she at least had a powder puff to remove its shininess.

"What's wrong with you?" she suddenly demanded, irritated with her angst.

She was clean and neat again. If Logan Crawford needed a social beauty for his boss, then he was on the wrong ranch. And she certainly wasn't going to force him to stay.

With her chin up, she marched down the stairs,

her mind focused on Aunt Beulah and her words of wisdom. She didn't need a man. She had cows.

But none of them looked as good as Logan Crawford.

Chapter Five

Melissa had introduced Logan to each of her daughters and offered him a glass of iced tea and some warm cookies.

"I wasn't sure you'd still be here," she said, an inquisitive smile on her lips.

Logan studied her. She was a beautiful woman, in a soft, feminine way. That thought startled him and he realized he was comparing her to Abby. When had he made Abby the measure by which he judged women?

"Uh, Abby and I agreed to a one-month trial. I helped her out today when she had a problem, and—"

"A problem?" Melissa interrupted, a frown on her face.

"Yeah, over on the Prine place."

Before Melissa could ask more questions, Abby entered the kitchen.

Logan knew at once that something had changed. Abby, after their agreement on his one-month trial, had been more relaxed than he'd seen her, almost accepting his presence. Now, her shoulders were rigid with tension and her lips were pressed into a straight line, though that bottom lip couldn't quite hide its fullness.

"Abby? You okay?" he asked without thinking.

She glowered at him. "Of course."

Melissa set a glass of tea on the table for her sister. "Let me get the girls settled in the den. Then we'll talk." She urged the three little girls to come watch a cartoon video in the den, accompanied by milk and fresh cookies.

As she escorted them from the kitchen, Logan said softly, under his breath, "I didn't mean to offend you. You looked upset."

She wouldn't look at him. Keeping her blue eyes shielded from him, she sipped her iced tea. "Nothing's wrong…other than what happened today."

Melissa came back in and grabbed her own glass before sitting down at the table. "You had trouble at the Prine place?"

This time Abby did look at him, but it was to accuse him of being a blabbermouth. "I was explaining why I'm still here."

Without responding to his words, she turned to her sister. "Pritchard cut the fences and the herd I had in the east pasture mingled with his, including his bull."

"Oh, no! Are you going to have him arrested?"

Abby gave a rueful smile, her full bottom lip back in evidence, which held Logan's gaze. "I don't have any proof he cut the wires, Melissa. But it's what I believe. I'm going to talk to the sheriff so he'll know what's going on, but I can't do anything else.''

Logan traced paths on the frosty sides of his glass of tea to avoid staring at Abby. She looked as young and fresh as a teenager with her scrubbed face. Which made her blue eyes stand out even more. Instead of the soft green of Melissa's eyes, Abby's were a dark blue, more compelling.

''What do you think, Logan?'' Melissa asked.

''What? Uh, what were you saying?'' he asked, hoping he was able to hide his embarrassment.

''Do you think Pritchard cut the wires?''

Logan cleared his throat. ''I don't know the man, but I know cut wires when I see them. Someone cut them, and he sure had an attitude when we got there.''

Abby added, ''We thought we'd talk to Wayne and see if his dad had any problems with the man in the past. He was looking for trouble.''

As Melissa checked the clock on the wall, they all heard voices on the front porch. ''Oh, good, they're here,'' Melissa announced. ''I thought it was about time for the bus. I'll get the other two to go to the den with the little ones.''

The next few minutes reminded Logan a lot of his younger days as Melissa skillfully maneuvered the three older children, giving them hugs, cookies and directions.

''Your sister's good,'' he said with a grin to Abby.

''She's the best,'' Abby agreed.

Strangely, however, Abby seemed more withdrawn than ever after their exchange. Clearly she loved her sister, so he didn't figure he'd upset her with his words. But something had.

The oldest boy came back into the kitchen with Melissa and she introduced him to Logan.

Logan rose and stretched out his hand, not surprised to have the boy shake it like a man. Kids on ranches grew up fast and Wayne was already fourteen.

"Wayne, we needed to ask you a question or two about your dad's place," Abby said as Melissa pushed the plate of cookies closer to the boy.

"Sure," he agreed as he devoured a cookie.

"Did he ever have any difficulty with Mr. Pritchard? Any disagreements or uneasy times?"

Wayne's chin rose. "Dad got along with everyone."

Logan leaned forward. "I'm sure he did, but did Pritchard ever offer to buy the place?"

"Yeah. A couple of times. Dad said he seemed real put out that Dad wouldn't sell." The boy stared down at the cookies in his hand. "Dad said he wanted to keep the place, to pass it down to his sons."

Abby reached out and put a hand on his shoulder. "And that's just what he did. You and Billy, and Susie, too, have a good future because of your dad."

Wayne looked up, pride in his gaze as he nodded at Abby.

"Did you ever find fences cut, or anything like that that you couldn't explain?" Logan asked, hoping for more information.

"No, I don't think so. Why? What happened?"

Logan wasn't sure how much Abby wanted to tell the kid, so he left the explanation to her. But she didn't keep anything back.

"If he did anything like that, Dad didn't mention it," Wayne said. "I'm sorry, Abby. What about the horses? Are they all right?"

Melissa grinned. "Abby would've told you if they weren't." Then she turned to Logan. "Wayne is almost as one-track about ProRide as Rob is. That's our rodeo supply business."

"I'm—I mean, me and Billy and Susie are part-owners," the boy added, his shoulders squaring with pride.

Logan grinned. "Profitable business, I've heard."

"Yeah. We started—"

"Now, don't get off track here," Melissa interrupted, a smile on her face. "Logan doesn't have all day to hear you rave about how great y'all are doing."

The boy blushed and ducked his head, but Logan tried to relieve his embarrassment. "Soon, I'd like you to show me what you're doing with it."

Abby, her mind still on what had happened, stood. "Thanks, Wayne, Melissa. I'm going to drive into town and talk to Sheriff Downy. When will Rob be back?"

"He hoped to get in late this evening. It's only two or three hours to Dallas."

"He's out of town?" Logan asked, surprised.

"He had to go down to the Mesquite Rodeo for a meeting. They're negotiating a contract for service."

"Yeah, they're a year-round operation, so it's an important contract," Wayne added.

Logan raised an eyebrow. He had been to the Mesquite Rodeo and knew it was a first-class operation. "You're right. I hope things go well."

Melissa smiled with pride. "Rob will manage."

Abby stopped walking once they reached the barn. "You don't have to go into town with me."

"I said I'd go."

"Fine. But I'm driving." She expected some argument. Logan seemed just like those men who thought they couldn't be driven by a woman. She headed for her truck and slid behind the wheel.

He said nothing as he got in beside her. At least without Floyd, they didn't have to ride close together. She was too distracted when the handsome cowboy was within touching distance. Not that she had anything to worry about. After comparing her to Melissa, she was sure he wasn't interested in her. She'd seen his gaze travel between the two of them.

"Sheriff Downy has been around here for a long time."

"Maybe he'll know whether there's been any trouble with Pritchard before."

"Or maybe he'll be best friends with him," Abby said dryly.

Logan frowned. "Is he?"

"I don't know. I haven't heard that, but I don't go into town all that much."

"You work too hard," he muttered.

Abby gave him a hard stare. "All ranchers work hard, if they're going to stay afloat."

She knew what he was going to say, and she held her breath, ready to attack. He was going to point out that she was a woman.

"Yeah, but that doesn't make it a good thing," he said and stared out the window of the truck.

She let out her pent-up breath.

"Wayne seems like a good kid," he said, changing the subject.

"He is. He worked like a Trojan all summer. Once school started, we all missed him." The Prine children were a safe subject, one that had no pitfalls.

"It's great that your sister and her husband took them in."

"Yes. Melissa and Rob are great parents."

"Don't you want to be a parent, a mother?"

So much for no pitfalls.

"I'm a rancher." She pressed down on the accelerator.

"Didn't mean to upset you," he muttered, his gaze fixed on the speed dial.

She eased up on the gas. "Don't be ridiculous. I'm not upset. But our family will have plenty of children without me contributing. After all, Beth is due in a few months, and Melissa already has six."

They had reached the outskirts of Tumbleweed, the closest town, while they talked, and Abby turned at the first intersection to reach the sheriff's office, one block from the main road.

They got out and entered the sparsely furnished office where a uniformed officer sat at a desk.

"Afternoon," Abby said. "I'm Abigail Kennedy

from the Circle K ranch. My manager, Logan Crawford. Is Sheriff Downy in?''

''I believe so, ma'am. I'll tell him you're here.''

Logan stood behind her, letting her take the lead.
She appreciated that. Some men—

''Come on back. The sheriff can see you,'' the
deputy called from halfway across the room.

He led them to an office at the back and gestured
for them to enter.

''Miz Abby,'' Sheriff Downy said, nodding at
her. Then he extended his hand to Logan. ''Mr.
Crawford. You connected to the Double C ranch in
Oklahoma?''

''My father's place,'' Logan said with a nod.

The man didn't show any irritation that his father's reputation preceded him, but Abby was beginning to understand his desire to make his own
way. It had taken her a couple of years before anyone would take her seriously as the head of the Circle K.

Even now, older men, like the sheriff, liked to
pretend that she wasn't in charge.

The sheriff gestured to the chairs in front of his
desk. ''What can I do for you folks?'' He looked at
Logan.

Logan turned to Abby and waited.

With a slight smile shot in his direction, she faced
the sheriff. ''We had a little trouble on the Prine
place this morning. Thought I'd keep you informed
in case things…escalate.''

''What kind of problem?'' Again the sheriff
looked at Logan.

Abby was tired of being ignored. She leaned forward, forcing the sheriff to look at her. "Some fence wires were cut, letting our herd mingle with Pritchard's."

"Now, Miz Abby, fences go down all the time. You know that."

"They certainly do. But these wires were cut," she said firmly.

"You saw someone cut them?"

"No."

"Well, then, you—"

"They were cut." Logan's voice was quiet but firm.

Sheriff Downy shifted his gaze. "You checked the wires?"

Logan looked at Abby, then back to the sheriff. "We *all* checked them. The cut was new. The fences had been checked only the week before. The wire was cut in two places, taking down about ten yards of fence."

The sheriff leaned back in his chair. "Well, now, you wantin' to bring charges? 'Cause without a witness, it could'a been anyone who—"

Abby was getting fed up with the man's attitude. He wouldn't accept her word, but Logan, a man he'd never met, could be believed?

Logan never looked at her. To the sheriff, he said, "It's not my decision."

Abby waited, saying nothing, until the sheriff returned his gaze to her. "No, I don't want to file charges. But Pritchard's attitude makes me think this won't be the last incident. I want to keep things peaceful, but I also want him to know I'm not stupid."

"Now, Miz Abby, no one would think—"

"That a woman doesn't know any better? Wrong, Sheriff. *Some* people don't take a woman rancher seriously." She kept her gaze firmly on him, knowing he got her meaning. "I'd like you to write up a report of our visit in case I have to come see you again."

"Well, of course I'll do that. I'll even ride out and visit with Pritchard, give him a little warning. But what about Duffy? Couldn't he maybe have an ax to grind?"

"And what ax would that be? He spent all morning helping us get the cattle back to our side of the pasture. That was a lot of work for an old man," Abby returned, fighting to keep her voice calm.

"I'm not accusing him," the sheriff hurriedly said. "But I've known Pritchard a long time. I don't think he'd do something underhanded like that."

"But you think Duffy would?" She drew a deep breath. "Pritchard wants to buy the Prine place."

"Nothing against the law about that," the sheriff said.

Abby rose. She'd had enough. "Write that report, Sheriff, and please send me a copy of it. I want it for my files."

Logan stood also, but he said nothing.

The sheriff sent her a hard look, as if to say he didn't like her telling him what to do. Then he extended his hand to Logan again, telling him he was pleased to meet him.

Abby kept quiet until they got in her truck. Then she only uttered one word as she squeezed the life out of the steering wheel. "Men!"

"Hey, not all of us are as bad as the sheriff."

She didn't respond for several minutes. Finally she said, "I appreciated your support in there."

He shrugged his shoulders. "I believe the wire was cut."

"I'm not talking about the wire. I'm talking about your not going along with the sheriff. You know he would've preferred talking to you and ignoring me."

Again he shrugged. "It's your ranch."

She dropped the subject, but the man beside her had risen in her estimation with his support. Maybe she hadn't made a mistake in hiring him after all.

Turning her thoughts to the problem at hand, she muttered, "Maybe I should go see Pritchard instead of waiting for the sheriff to do so."

She was scarcely aware she'd spoken her thoughts aloud until Logan cleared his throat.

"Uh, Abby, maybe you should wait until Rob gets home and let him handle this. Or see if Jed would do it."

She glared at him. So much for thinking she hadn't made a mistake.

Logan knew Abby was upset with him again. She definitely didn't have a poker face. He caught himself tracing her profile as she stared stonily ahead.

"I didn't mean...Pritchard is a hard nut. He won't—"

"Listen to a woman? Not many men will," she snapped.

Logan gave up with a sigh. When she got her dander up, there was no reasoning with her. Besides, she transferred her anger to the gas pedal.

Gradually she slowed down to normal speeds, a frown on her face. He thought of how careful his mother was to never create wrinkles. She stayed in the shade and creamed her face religiously.

Yet Abby's skin, with its light tan, looked soft and smooth. Touchable.

He stiffened at that thought. He was forgetting she was his boss. For a month. If she could read his mind, he'd be off the ranch in the blink of an eye.

That wasn't what he wanted.

"Reckon Ellen will have dinner ready when we get home?" he asked, looking for a neutral subject.

Abby checked her watch. "Probably. It's almost six. I guess I can put off seeing Pritchard until after dinner."

"Abby—"

"I'm in charge, Logan. I'll make the decision about what should be done."

Her voice was cold, hard.

Enough said. He wasn't going to change her mind. But maybe he could convince her to let him tag along. He didn't like the idea of her going out after dark by herself.

A chuckle escaped him as he thought about how Abby would react to that sentiment.

"What's funny? You think it's amusing that I'm in charge of the ranch?" she demanded, her voice tight with tension.

"Nope! I was laughing at—at myself, worrying about you being out after dark."

"What?"

"Females in my family don't—the world's a dangerous place."

"And you believe every woman needs a big, strong man to protect her?" She continued to stare straight ahead, but Logan thought she had steam coming out of her ears.

"Well, it doesn't hurt. Women can be the target of many a man's anger...or lust. There's no point in taking chances." His father had always pointed out his sons' responsibility to protect their mother and sister.

"The women in your family must live a very restricted life."

"They're very happy with their lives. They have everything they want."

"Except their freedom." Her chin was up in the air and she shot him a look of contempt. "How old is your sister?"

"Nineteen." Then he added, "She was a late baby. She's seven years younger than my youngest brother."

"And she considers it normal to be hemmed in by men?"

Logan drew a deep breath. This conversation, if one could call it that, was threatening to get out of control. "I didn't mean—we're protecting her, not stopping her from doing anything she wants to do. If she wants to go somewhere at night, one of us goes with her."

"That must make it easy for her to pick up guys," Abby drawled.

"Is that what you do? Go out at night by yourself and pick up men?" he demanded, a flare of jealousy he'd never felt before consuming him.

"That's none of your business. Which is my point."

"Damn it, Abby, why are we arguing about this? My sister is perfectly happy with things the way they are. And I have no intention of intruding on your private...entertainment." But he wanted to. He didn't want to let her out of his sight.

To protect her, of course. That was all.

"Good. Because if you did, I'd have to back out of our agreement."

He folded his arms over his chest and stared straight ahead.

Chapter Six

Well, the line had been drawn.

If Logan crossed it, he'd be fired. She had made that clear. He watched her at dinner. She joined in the conversation, what little there was, giving nothing away. But she didn't mellow out. There was still some fire in her gaze.

Maybe he could convince Floyd to go with her. He was pretty sure she wouldn't let *him* accompany her.

He was so busy worrying over what would happen later, he scarcely tasted the chocolate cake Ellen had baked. When the phone rang as they were finishing up, he breathed a sigh of relief when he realized it was Rob. He'd gotten back to the ranch.

"Sure, come on over, Rob," Abby said, her voice pleasant.

Logan immediately tried to come up with a reason to hang around and grab a minute of Rob's time.

Rob would understand that Abby needed a man to go with her to talk to Pritchard.

"Uh, Abby, can you go over what you want done tomorrow?" he asked.

"I want us to do the artificial insemination on that herd we rounded up today. The vet is scheduled to be here at seven in the morning."

He nodded. "With all four of us assisting him, we should be through by noon. Then shall—"

"Four? Five of us. All five of us will assist."

He frowned. "But Abby—"

"Are you going to tell me it's unladylike for me to be present?" she asked, her voice rising.

That was exactly what he'd been going to say, or, at least, something similar. Maybe he'd have used the word appropriate rather than unladylike. But—

"Forget it, Logan. I'm not a lady. I'm a rancher!"

"And a good one," Floyd said, patting her on the shoulder. "The boy didn't mean anything. He thought you might have other work to do. Like all that paperwork you're always complaining about."

The old cowboy winked at Logan, and he nodded in thanks.

"Paperwork is for when it's dark." Abby picked up her dishes and carried them to the sink.

Logan hid his smile. She sounded just like his father. The man worked tirelessly, even when his sons urged him to slow down.

A knock on the back door announced Rob's arrival. But if Logan thought he'd have a chance to join the conversation, Abby put an end to that by inviting Rob into her office.

With a frown on his face, he thanked Ellen for

the dinner and strolled outside. Dusk was falling and the air was chilly. He hadn't worn a jacket and he felt the crispness of the wind through his work shirt.

But he couldn't go to the bunkhouse yet. He had to talk to Rob first. Pulling his cell phone off his belt, he dialed the number for the Double C, his home.

"Hello? Double C."

"Lindsay?"

"Logan! When are you coming home?"

He and his little sister had a special relationship. He missed her. "Not for a while, baby. I've been hired on here at the Circle K near Wichita Falls."

"Oh. I've missed you."

"I've missed you, too. How's everything going around there?"

"The ranch is fine. I know that's what you're asking about. But I'm not! Dad's being impossible."

"About what?"

"I met this guy, and Dad won't let me go out with him. There's nothing wrong with him, Logan. He's Mary Ellen's cousin from Dallas. We were all going to go to the state fair in Oklahoma City, and Dad said one of you guys has to go with me. I'm not a baby!"

"I'm sure he doesn't think you are," Logan soothed, but suddenly he started looking at the situation from Abby's point of view. Were they being too restrictive with his sister? He shook his head, hating the thought of letting her go out with some strange man.

"But it's not fair!"

"Baby, you can't—"

"I'm not a baby!"

The back door opened and Rob appeared. Logan quickly promised to call back later and hung up on his sister's protests.

"Rob?" he called and strode across the yard to catch up with the other man.

"Yeah, Logan. Glad you're staying, by the way. Melissa told me."

"Yeah. Uh, did Abby talk to you about visiting Pritchard?"

"You mean today's incident?"

"No, I mean going to see him tonight."

Rob came to an abrupt halt. "What are you talking about?"

"Earlier, she said she thought she'd go have a talk with Pritchard about what happened today, and her suspicions that he may have cut the fence."

"No, she didn't mention doing that," Rob said thoughtfully, frowning. "But it might be a good idea, to get it all out in the open."

"So you'll go with her?"

Rob turned to stare at him. "Not unless she asks me."

Logan was flabbergasted. He'd thought Rob was a reasonable man, a smart man. "But you can't let her—"

Rob chuckled. "Haven't you figured out yet that Abby's an independent woman?"

"Yeah, but there's no reason to put herself in danger!" Logan exploded.

Rob raised one eyebrow. "You think Pritchard would hurt her?"

"No, but—" Logan broke off. What he really

thought was that Pritchard would be difficult, unpleasant. He'd try to intimidate Abby.

The kitchen door opened, then closed, and Logan knew without turning around that Abby had come outside. He slowly turned to stare at her.

She was still dressed in jeans and boots, but she'd rebraided her long, dark hair, looking neat and tidy. The sudden urge to see her without her hair tied up, hanging like a dark curtain down her back, took his breath away.

"Rob? Is there a problem?"

Logan noticed she didn't speak to him.

"No problem, Abby. You going out?" Rob asked, covering the fact that Logan had revealed her intent.

"I'm going over to have a chat with Pritchard," she said, her voice as cool as the evening air.

"Want some company?"

Abby glared at Logan before she turned to Rob. "No, thanks. I don't want a testosterone-filled confrontation."

"Okay. Let me know how it works out." Rob's voice was calm, accepting.

Logan practically had to bite his tongue to stop from ordering her back into the house. This was crazy. A slim, beautiful young woman was going to confront a big bear of a man like Pritchard? A man who had already shown himself to be dishonorable?

The two men stood there in silence as Abby crossed to her pickup and got in. When the door had closed, ensuring she couldn't hear him, Logan said, "I can't believe you're letting her go have a face-off without any backup."

Rob shrugged his shoulders. "She'll be all right."
He paused, then added, "You going to wait up to
make sure she gets in okay?"

"Of course I am!" Logan snapped. Like he'd get
any sleep until she returned.

"Good. Then I won't have to worry. 'Night, Logan. Glad you're staying."

He walked toward his house, leaving Logan
standing there, worried and frustrated.

Abby turned into the Circle K driveway with a
sigh of relief. Her day was almost over. She
wouldn't do any office work tonight. No, she'd in-
dulge herself with a bubble bath, a long soak in
warm water, soothing her sore muscles and her ach-
ing head.

Her interview with Pritchard hadn't been pleasant.
The man was ornery, determined to purchase the
Prine ranch. Abby had patiently explained why the
ranch would not be put on the market. No matter
what happened.

Pritchard had countered with an above-the-market
offer, emphasizing that the amount, invested, would
probably bring the Prine children a better future than
hanging on to the land.

She pulled the truck to a halt by the barn, where
she usually parked, and turned off the engine and
lights. Then she leaned back with a sigh, staring at
the peaceful scene before her.

Her counter to Pritchard's point was simple. The
children needed the link to their parents, not money.
Money was cold consolation to their heritage.

She'd give up her inheritance if she could have

Aunt Beulah back, even at her most irascible. Abby, more than her two sisters, had found in Aunt Beulah the replacement for her parents. Now she was alone.

Not really, of course. She had both her sisters and their families. But they were all living their own lives. She opened the truck door and slid out. She doubted that she'd satisfied Pritchard, but she'd given him something to think about.

Trudging to the back porch, she came to an abrupt halt when one of the shadows stood. In spite of her voice shaking, she demanded, "Who's there?"

"Me," a deep voice said softly.

She recognized Logan's voice at once. Or maybe it was his scent. Logan Crawford had a distinct aroma that made her fantasize about silk sheets, moonlight...

"What are you doing here?" she said, her voice firmer now that she'd identified the shadow.

"Waiting for you."

An unexpected warmth filled her even as she protested. "You thought I'd need your help?"

"I wanted to hear how things went."

Okay, she could accept curiosity. Suddenly feeling weak, she sank down on the porch where he'd been sitting. He joined her, his closeness causing her to gasp for air.

"He—he didn't admit anything. But I explained to him that the land wouldn't be sold, no matter what. He tried to persuade me that it was in the best interest of the kids to sell it. He offered a lot of money."

She named the sum and Logan whistled. "That's a good price."

"Yes. But it doesn't matter. Wayne won't agree to sell."

"Rob and Melissa could decide to do that for him. I'm sure they're the guardians since they're adopting the kids."

Abby took in another deep breath of the sweet, cool night air. "They won't. Rob understands the importance of keeping the land. He had to sell his father's place when he died."

Logan nodded, saying nothing else.

He understood, too, Abby knew. She'd heard it in his voice, that pride of ownership when he talked about his father's ranch. "I hope I convinced him."

"Was he rude?"

Abby chuckled, finding the meeting humorous now that she was no longer dealing with her neighbor. "It wasn't exactly a tea party."

"That's why I didn't want you to go alone," Logan muttered.

"Afraid I'd melt if the man said boo? I'm tougher than that, Logan. I'm not like the women in your family." She regretted the scorn in her voice. "I didn't mean—"

"I may have misled you. My mother isn't considered weak by anyone who knows her. But she prefers to avoid unpleasantness. Most people do."

She apologized again. "I didn't mean to insult anyone. Pritchard *was* unpleasant, but not unbearably so." She'd already apologized. She might as well go all the way. Aunt Beulah had taught her to be honest. "And I appreciate your concern. I really do. But I'm used to managing on my own."

"I gathered that," he said dryly and stood.

She rose also, suddenly reluctant to let him go. "Are you going to move into the manager's house?"

He shook his head. "Don't see any point. At least, not for a month."

A month. The time she'd given him to prove himself. To prove they could work together.

"I'm sure—" she began, wanting to encourage him to settle in. Already, she found herself enjoying having someone she could rely on to take care of things.

"I don't want to have to move twice." With an abrupt nod she barely saw in the darkness, he strode away without saying good-night.

"Well, you managed to chase him away, didn't you, Abigail?" she muttered.

Just as well. The attraction she was feeling for the man was too tempting. And she already knew how it would turn out. She wouldn't be woman enough for him.

He'd look for a woman like his mother. Or his sister. One who liked being taken care of. One who knew her place in his life. One who wore a frilly apron and waited on him when he came in at night.

Someone like Melissa.

But not like her.

Logan quietly eased his way into the bunkhouse. He didn't want conversation with the other men, even if they were awake.

He'd come back earlier and put on a blue-jean jacket lined with lambswool to stay warm while he maintained his vigil. When Abby had returned, relief had flooded him, releasing the tension that had made his body sore.

The relief had been so great, he'd wanted to haul her into his arms, hold her close, kiss away the exhaustion he saw on her face. Instead he'd kept his hands to himself, only allowing himself to sit next to her, close enough to inhale her scent, but not to touch.

He was walking a tightrope here. One wrong move and he figured she'd fire him. And every day, it was growing more and more important that he be allowed to stay.

Because he liked the setup, he hurriedly assured himself. The ranch was well-run. The people were friendly. The weather—aw, hell. The boss was a beauty who tempted him beyond belief.

He'd seen other good ranches. He'd worked with good people. But he'd never been tempted to fondle the boss. To stroke her dark hair, pushing his fingers through the silken strands. To caress her pouty bottom lip. Just thinking about that mouth was driving him insane.

And yet, she confused him. On the one hand, he saw her as a beautiful woman. On the other, she was a more than competent cowboy, a skilled and tireless worker. Even more than that, she did a bang-up job running the ranch. She made the decisions that kept it in the black, a growing and expanding empire.

In his family, gender roles were well-defined. His father took care of the outdoors, his mother the indoors. Each ran his or her world with a firm hand. His mother wasn't weak. But she never crossed the line into the man's world.

He wondered what would have happened had his mother been left a widow, as Abby's aunt had been, with no sons to take over the masculine roles. He'd never questioned his family's take on the world until he'd arrived at the Circle K.

His admiration for Abby Kennedy was based on more than her beauty. In his eyes, she was beautiful, though he realized, looking at her sisters, that others might consider them prettier. But, strangely enough, it was Abby's strength that drew him, too.

Drew him and repelled him.

She was like an exotic bird, among the wrens of the world. Soft, feminine women were the norm in his world. He and his brothers had been pursued by young women from high school on. Whether because of their physical assets or their financial ones, the boys had had their choice of beautiful women.

His mother had been urging them to marry for a long time. Yet, none of them had done so. For Logan, his perception of marriage, fostered by his parents, was one of the man choosing a woman to care for. To shelter. To provide all her worldly wants.

A woman, while giving him pleasure, would demand a lot of time away from his world. He hated the social functions his mother insisted her sons attend. He wasn't anxious to be forced to spend even more time in such pursuits.

Now he'd found a woman who lived in his world, not his mother's. He was resisting the attraction as best he could. He'd told himself he wasn't ready to settle down. But he was fascinated with her strengths.

Her lack of need of *his* strengths also confused

him. Man was supposed to be the strong one. Woman was the nester, the weak one who needed to be protected.

Not Abby Kennedy.

Tonight, she hadn't needed him to wait up for her. To be there when she got home. To listen to the events of the evening. *He* had been the one with the need. *He* had been the one who couldn't sleep without that few minutes in the shadows. *He* had been the one longing to hold her close.

Life was suddenly a lot more confusing than it had ever been before. And a little scary.

He didn't know what to do.

After breakfast the next morning, Logan and the cowboys loaded a portable shoot onto the back of Abby's pickup. Then they filled Logan's horse trailer with four mounts.

"I gotta get that flat fixed," Floyd muttered, "or Abby's gonna kill me."

Logan grinned at him. "Probably, but four horses are all we need this morning. Someone will have to assist the doc."

"Yeah," Floyd agreed. "Usually that's Barney."

"Not Abby? I thought that job would be easier—"

"Boy, you got to stop making those remarks," Floyd hurriedly said, looking over his shoulder. "If Abby hears you say she's not able to get the job done, you'll be in hot water."

"Hot water might feel good this morning," Dirk muttered as he closed the gate to the horse trailer.

The wind was sharper this morning. Ellen announced over breakfast that a cold front was approaching.

"Not that kind," Logan muttered. Abby hadn't spoken to him this morning. He figured she was mad at him for waiting up for her last night.

"Here she comes," Floyd whispered.

Logan turned to stare at her as she crossed the distance between the house and barn. Her hat was pulled low and her jacket collar turned up, her hands in the coat pockets. But he wouldn't mistake her for a cowboy. Her walk, in form-fitting jeans, identified her.

Barney was walking with her, talking while she listened. Her gaze was checking their work.

When she reached them, she asked, "Are the horses loaded? Did you load Ruby?"

Floyd stepped forward. "'Course, Abby, she's in there."

"Good. Let's get started. I think we're going to be ready for a hot meal at lunchtime." She strode to her pickup and slid behind the wheel.

Logan moved to his own truck. Floyd and Dirk got in with him, and Barney rode with Abby. The vet, in his own truck, was waiting at the gate to the Prine place and joined their procession. When they reached the east pasture, the four men lifted out the portable shoot. Abby and the vet stood talking in easy comradeship that caught Logan's eye.

"Good vet?" he asked Floyd.

"Yeah. Hard worker."

"Married?"

Floyd's head swung around and he stared at Logan. "Why?"

Logan shrugged, trying to make his question look casual. "Just wondered."

There was a grin on Floyd's face that irritated Logan, but he waited in silence for his answer.

"Yeah, he's married. Abby is friends with his wife."

Good. Not that it mattered, he assured himself, but it helped to know relationships in a new situation. He started unloading the horses. When all the men were mounted, he led them toward the cows that were grazing nearby. "We'll start with these. Let's begin pushing them up. Barney, if you're going to assist the vet, give your mount to Abby as soon as we get the first ones there."

The teamwork felt good. As the morning progressed, Logan was pleased with the rapidity of their work. The vet was efficient. Dirk and Floyd brought up the cows and he and Abby drove them one at a time to the chute. Barney assisted the vet, then made a mark on the cow's hide with a black marker, so they'd know which cows had been treated, before releasing it.

About ten o'clock, the sleet, mixed with rain, started. They pulled their hats lower and made sure their collars were up. Logan wanted to tell Abby to go sit in her truck until they were finished. But he knew better.

Besides, she was a skilled cowhand.

They only had about twenty-five head left to do, in his estimation, when the vet's cell phone rang.

The vet left the chute, jogging toward Abby. "I'm going to have to go. A truckload of horses went off the road because of the ice. There are a lot of in-juries.''

"Okay," Abby agreed, a worried frown on her forehead.

Logan urged his mount closer. "If you'll leave me the equipment, I can finish up. We'll bring it to your office afterward."

"You've done this before?" the vet asked.

"Yeah. I'm from the Double C ranch in Oklahoma. We've been doing it ourselves for a while."

"Okay with you, Abby?" the vet asked.

"Yeah. I don't want to have to try to do this again when the marker might've worn off."

Logan swung out of the saddle and tied his horse to the trailer, before taking the tube gun from the doctor.

The man slapped him on the shoulder before say-ing, "Okay, the future babies of the Circle K are in your hands." Then he hurried away to his truck.

Logan stared at Abby, thinking about a different kind of future baby of the Circle K. Suddenly he wasn't cold anymore.

Chapter Seven

Abby didn't understand the strange look Logan gave her. "You sure you're okay with this?"

Relief filled her at his abrupt nod. He turned his back on her and approached the cow trapped in the chute.

Abby turned her attention to cutting out the next cow and forcing her to the chute. It was a lot harder to do with only one rider. When Floyd rode up beside her, she gave him a smile of thanks.

"Can Dirk manage by himself?"

"You bet."

Which meant they'd all get out of the weather that much faster. The sleet was coming down faster, stinging their faces if they didn't stay covered. Abby was shivering as she struggled to stay in her saddle.

Within the hour, they were finished. By the time the last cow was released, the others had loaded the four horses in Logan's trailer.

"Leave the chute," Abby ordered. "We'll get it another time. Everybody in the trucks and let's get out of here while we still can."

No one argued. Just being out of the wind, with other warm bodies, brought a little relief to all of them. But they were almost home before the trucks warmed up enough for the heaters to help.

"Man, I hope Ellen has something hot ready," Barney muttered. "I think every inch of me is frozen."

"The wind was sharp," Abby agreed. She wasn't sure the actual temperature was below freezing, but the strength of the wind probably brought the wind-chill factor down.

When they'd parked the trucks, Abby hurried to Logan's trailer to help with the horses.

"We've got them, Abby. Go on up to the house," Logan shouted over the storm.

The other men nodded and Abby surprised herself by agreeing. She didn't make it any easier on herself than she did her men, normally. But there were four horses and four men. They didn't need her.

She turned and started for the house.

That was when she noticed the strange vehicle parked nearby. Who was visiting in this kind of weather? Someone who drove an expensive sports car.

When she opened the back door, a blast of warm air hit her and sent shivers all over her body. She was barely inside the door, when Ellen greeted her with a cup of hot coffee.

"Get this inside you," she ordered. "Where are the others?"

"They're putting up the horses. They'll be here in a minute," she assured her housekeeper. "Whose car is—"

Before she could finish, a young woman hurried into the kitchen. "I think they're back, Ellen," she said before realizing Abby was there. "Oh!"

"They are," Ellen agreed. "Lindsay, this Abby Kennedy. Abby, Lindsay Crawford."

Abby choked on her coffee. "Crawford? You're Logan's sister?"

"Yes," the young woman agreed, a smile on her pretty face.

She was shorter than Abby by several inches and dressed in designer fleece pants and long-sleeved top, her hair expertly cut. Definitely high maintenance.

"Uh, did Logan know you were coming?"

"No, I wanted to surprise him. Do you mind?" She looked anxious.

"No, of course not. Uh, I think I'll go wash up," she informed Ellen, but her gaze remained on the young woman. She headed for the stairs, but the sound of boots on the porch had her slowing down. Somehow, she wanted to see Logan's reaction to his sister's arrival.

The back door opened and a gust of cold wind entered with the four men. Ellen was pouring cups of coffee and they headed to the counter to wrap their frozen hands around the stone mugs.

"Logan?"

The soft, feminine voice stopped all four men.

Abby watched as disbelief, chased by pleasure

and then consternation filled Logan's face. He crossed the room and hugged his sister.

"Ooh, you're cold and you smell like cows!"

"Hardly surprising, baby. What are you doing here?"

"I wanted to see you."

"Do Mom and Dad know you're here?"

Abby's gaze collided with Ellen's and she decided her housekeeper could handle everything. With a murmured "Excuse me," she headed for the stairs.

Logan went to the workroom with the rest of the men to clean up, leaving his sister with Ellen.

"Your stacks of laundry are in there folded. You could probably find some dry clothes to change into," the housekeeper called as they shut the door.

Barney and Dirk immediately grabbed dry clothing and started stripping. Floyd had gone to his and Ellen's apartment that connected to the kitchen.

"Ain't you going to change?" Barney asked, bringing Logan back to an awareness of his surroundings.

"Uh, yeah," he agreed, reaching for the stack of clean clothes that he recognized.

"Ellen takes good care of us," Barney added.

Logan nodded, but he didn't have anything to say. His mind was still dealing with the appearance of his sister. He'd only talked to her yesterday. He'd had no idea she'd appear at the ranch.

The sound of sleet on the windows reminded him that she wouldn't be leaving anytime soon. What was he going to do with her?

And she hadn't answered his question about whether his parents knew where she was. If they didn't, he'd have to call them at once.

"Hey, man, hurry up. You know Ellen won't serve until we're all at the table," Barney urged.

When the three men emerged from the workroom, having washed and donned dry clothes, they discovered the three women all in the kitchen. Abby had also changed, but she still wore work clothes, jeans and a shirt.

Lindsay, next to her, looked like a lady of leisure. Logan knew his sister was attending class at the local college, but he'd have to admit she didn't work at a job. Instead his father gave her an allowance that more than took care of her needs.

"Lindsay, you did tell Mom and Dad you were coming here, didn't you?"

His sister ignored his question, as did Ellen. "Everyone sit down. Lunch is ready." She began dishing up big bowls of a fragrant beef stew.

Logan felt like he had no choice. He certainly couldn't hold up everyone's meal. But he grabbed a chair next to his sister.

Leaning toward her, he demanded harshly, "Answer my question."

"No, they don't know," she ripped back. "Satisfied?" She passed a bowl of the stew to him with a fake smile.

He frowned. "Where did you tell them you were going?"

"To school. But I cut classes and came here instead," she whispered.

He abruptly stood. "Abby, excuse me, but I need

to go call my parents. They're probably going crazy looking for my sister."

Lindsay stopped him. "Really, Logan, you know I wouldn't make them worry. I have my cell phone with me. They called me a couple of hours ago and told me to stay in town. They said it was too dangerous to drive. I promised I wouldn't start home." She sent him a triumphant smile.

Abby smiled at his sister, then turned to Logan. "It seems the problem is taken care of, Logan. Eat your stew."

Frustrated, Logan fell back into his chair. Pulling the bowl of stew closer to him, he began eating. Women! What else could he do?

Abby hid her smile behind a bite of stew. Logan's sister was obviously protected and provided for, but she hadn't allowed the protection to stop her from doing what she wanted.

And she'd frustrated her brother.

Abby waited until her men were warm and well-fed before she announced their chore for the afternoon.

"I know it's miserable weather—and you can have the afternoon off as soon as you load the truck with hay."

"Why?" Logan snapped, turning to her in surprise.

His attention had been focused on his sister most of the meal. Now he stared at Abby as if she was a stranger. Maybe she was, Abby thought, compared to the beautiful and feminine Lindsay.

"I'm going to put out hay for the herd in the

south pasture. I'd planned on moving them this afternoon because that pasture is about played out, but with the weather so bad, I'll feed them today and move them when the storm lets up.''

"By yourself? Don't be ridiculous. The men and I will take care of it,'' he assured her, as if the matter were settled.

Abby was warmed by the men's nods, showing their willingness to spend the afternoon out in bad weather for her sake. She gave them an appreciative smile until her gaze reached Logan. Then her voice turned as cold as the wind that had frozen them that morning. "That is my decision, Logan.''

"Even if the weather weren't a factor, going out by yourself would be foolish. Going out when there's no need is ridiculous.''

"The cows might disagree with you,'' Abby muttered and stood to carry her dishes to the sink.

"I didn't mean the cows shouldn't be fed, and you know it,'' Logan growled. "But there's no need for *you* to do it.''

Abby gave him a hard stare before she turned back to the table. "I think about twenty-five bales will do, guys.'' Then she hurried upstairs to find the wool muffler she'd gotten as a gift from Melissa last Christmas.

When she came back down, only Ellen and Lindsay were still in the kitchen.

"Did they go down to the barn?'' Abby asked as she strode through the room.

"Yes,'' Ellen assured her.

"You made Logan mad,'' Lindsay added.

Abby raised an eyebrow. "Really? It probably

won't be the last time. He has trouble following orders.''

As she shrugged on her coat, she watched Lindsay's eyes widen in surprise.

''You're his boss?''

''Yes, I am. It's my ranch.''

Lindsay's surprise disappeared in an infectious giggle. ''Poor Logan.''

Abby looked at her in surprise.

''Oh, I didn't mean—it's just that he's not used to a woman being in charge.''

''Well, he's got a month to adjust,'' Abby said, grinning in return. Then she settled her hat on her head, pulled on her gloves and stepped out into the elements.

When she reached the barn, the four men had almost finished lofting the heavy bales into the back of her truck. She stepped inside the barn to grab a pair of wire cutters.

When she emerged, they'd finished. ''Thanks, guys. I'll see you at dinner.''

Without argument, they headed for the bunkhouse. Only Logan remained.

She reached for the truck door, but he put his gloved hand over hers.

''Want me to drive?''

''Why would you drive when you're not even going?''

''I'm going, Abby, whether you like it or not. It's not safe for someone to go out alone on a day like today. If the truck slipped into a ditch or something, you'd be alone.''

She glared at him. "If the truck slips into a ditch, I'd call for help. It only takes one to telephone."

"And if the call won't go through because of the elements?"

"I don't see how two of us freezing to death is better than one of us."

"With two of us, we can share our body heat," he pointed out, a grin on his lips that brought a blush to her cheeks.

She ducked her head and pushed against his chest. "I'm driving. And I don't need any help."

Instead of answering her, he strode around to the passenger side of the truck and swung inside.

"You are very hardheaded," she muttered as she closed the door behind her.

"Me? You're the one who keeps insisting on going out when you don't need to. Any of the men would've volunteered to go with me, and you know it."

"None of them are young anymore. They give all they can every day. I didn't want to ask too much," she explained, a frown on her face. Barney suffered from arthritis, though he tried to hide it. Dirk was almost as old and the cold weather affected him as well.

Floyd was younger and in better shape, but Abby worried about him, too. Ellen was so happy these days, since she'd married him.

"You worry about everyone but yourself," Logan growled.

His sister's image popped into her head. "I suppose you don't worry about anyone? How about your sister? Do you worry about her?"

"Of course I do. I'm supposed to take care of her."

Abby shook her head but said nothing else. She wasn't going to be able to convince this man that his sister could take care of herself. And maybe she couldn't, since she'd been hovered over all her life.

But Aunt Beulah had raised Abby and her sisters to take care of themselves. She didn't need a Sir Galahad to help her feed her cows.

Logan jumped out and opened the two gates they had to go through. Each time he got back in the truck, he was covered with ice.

"I think it's getting worse," he muttered the second time. "The temperature is dropping."

She nodded. The driving had gotten a little trickier, too, but she hadn't said anything. When they reached the herd, Logan reached for his door handle again.

"Wait. I'll throw out the hay if you'll drive the truck," she said.

He rolled his eyes in exasperation. "I'm the one who's going to throw out the hay, Abby. You do the driving."

She considered arguing with him again, but his offer was a good one. "At least wear this if you're going to stay out there," she said, holding out her muffler.

He frowned. "What do you expect me to do with that?"

The sheer wool muffler was a hot-pink, not a color most men would choose.

"I expect you to wrap it around the bottom half of your face so you won't freeze." He continued to stare first at it and then her. "Here," she said, leaning toward him and looping the muffler around his neck.

"Hey!" he protested.

"Quit fussing," she said, unable to hold back a smile. For once, the cowboy wasn't in charge. She wrapped the muffler over the bottom half of his face, thinking it was a shame to cover those lips.

She had to lean closer to tie the muffler behind his neck. He reached out, his hands sliding up under her arms, taking her by surprise. Her breathing sped up and she jerked back. A warm tingling raced along her skin. "What are you doing?"

"I thought you might lose your balance," he assured her, his voice muffled through the wool.

"We need to get the hay put out," she muttered, turning back to the steering wheel.

"Right."

He climbed into the back of the truck and began clipping wires, releasing the baled hay. As she drove slowly around the pasture, he threw out the hay. Cows began to follow the truck, in spite of the sleet.

When the hay was all distributed, he crawled back into the cab of the truck, sleet covering his jacket, hat and the pink muffler.

Abby knew he'd saved her from being in the same state. She leaned toward him to untie the muffler.

As it slipped down around his neck, he muttered, "Thanks, it helped."

"You're welcome. Thanks for putting out the hay."

He grinned, a heartwarming, teasing smile that had her heart racing. "Thanks for letting me."

"I think you're getting carried away. Thanking me for letting you turn yourself into a Popsicle is ridiculous."

His smile widened. "Yeah."

Abby realized her hands were resting on his chest and she jerked them back. "We'd better start back."

"Yeah," he repeated, pulling the muffler from his neck and brushing the ice from his coat.

Abby turned the truck around and started back on the path they'd followed, but it was difficult to see as the sleet covered up their earlier tracks.

"Uh, Abby, Lindsay isn't going to be able to get back home tonight. Would you be able to put her up? Since I'm in the bunkhouse—"

"Ellen's already fixed a room for her."

"Thanks," he said with a sigh of relief.

"Did you really think I'd throw her out in this kind of weather?" She took her gaze from the pasture to look at him.

"No, but I felt bad about asking."

"I've got plenty of room."

They hit something under the sleet and the back of the truck slid out. Abby brought the truck back under control and doubled her concentration on her driving.

Up ahead lay the portion of the drive that worried her. A small creek ran across the pastures less than a mile from the house. The water level wasn't deep, but the sides of the creek were steep. As slippery as the pasture was becoming, she wasn't sure she could get the truck up the other side of the creek.

As if he read her mind, Logan said, "Will we be able to make it?"

She glanced at him before turning back to her driving. "I don't know. Are you warming up?"

"Sure. It beats riding in the back."

She gave him a faint smile, but she didn't say anything. The creek was coming up. "I'm going to have to go faster than I want if we're going to get up the other side. Brace yourself."

He stretched one arm along the back of the seat and put his other hand on the dashboard. When she looked his way again, he gave her an encouraging smile.

That simple gesture touched her. In spite of his having wanted her to stay out of the storm, he was putting his trust in her to get them back.

As they approached the creek, she pressed down on the accelerator, hoping to build enough speed to take them up the other side before the ice stopped them.

Bouncing over the rough, slick ground down the side of the creek, Abby pressed even harder on the accelerator. But she knew. Before the truck had actually slid to a halt, she knew she'd lost the battle.

Halfway up the other side, they lost traction and the truck began to slide back down to the creek. The vehicle rocked and jerked to one side before coming to rest against a large rock.

"That'll mean a new paint job," Logan said, his drawl calm.

Abby drew a deep breath. "Are you all right?"

"Yeah, I'm fine. Nice try. You almost made it."

"Not really," she admitted with a sigh. She reached in her coat pocket for the cell phone she carried. But, as Logan had predicted, the storm made it impossible to get a call through.

"Looks like there won't be a calvary to the rescue," she said, putting the phone back in her pocket. "If we wait long enough, I'm sure someone will come after us."

"By then, we probably *will* be Popsicles, unless we share a lot of body heat," he said, grinning at her.

The shiver that rolled through her body wasn't caused by the cold. The thought of getting close enough to Logan to share their body heat wasn't something she could contemplate calmly.

"I suggest we walk back to the house. It's less than a mile."

Abby just hoped that a walk in the storm would be able to cool her heated skin…and thoughts. But she didn't think it would.

Chapter Eight

Logan stared at Abby, thinking about the trek ahead of them. "You're sure? I think we could keep each other warm until Floyd comes for us."

"I'm sure. It's another couple of hours before he'd get here. We can be there in half an hour," she assured him, but he noticed she didn't meet his gaze.

More like an hour, he estimated. As long as they didn't get lost, they should be okay. They were both warmly dressed and in good condition. "Okay," he agreed, without challenging her statement.

She took a deep breath, as if gathering her strength. "Do you have a knife?"

"A knife? What for?" he demanded, wondering if there was a problem he hadn't foreseen.

"We can cut my muffler in half and both use it."

He frowned. "I don't want to destroy it. You use it. I'll be fine."

She shook her head. "No, it can be replaced. We

need every help we can get.'' She held out her hand and waited.

He slowly reached into his jeans pocket for the knife he always carried, vowing that he'd find a muffler to replace Abby's. Placing his knife in Abby's hand, he then held the muffler as she indicated. With a sawing motion, she cut the muffler in two.

"If you put the ends under your hat, it should stay in place,'' she advised, looping her half of the muffler over her face like a harem mask.

Logan quickly covered the bottom half of his face before she could see his smile. Abby wouldn't be a compliant member of a harem. She'd have the women organized and attacking their benefactor before he knew what was happening.

All thoughts of a desert harem disappeared when they opened the truck doors and staggered out into the fierce wind and stinging sleet. The first few steps up the side of the creek were the most difficult. When Abby slipped, Logan quickly backed her up, helping her reach the top.

She offered him a hand for his last step, returning his favor. When they were both upright, she lifted her arm to indicate the direction they needed to go. And the struggle began.

They hadn't gone far before Logan's arm looped around Abby's shoulders, pulling them close together. Though she lifted her head, her eyes flashing her surprise, she didn't pull away.

He told himself he was only trying to protect Abby, to make the walk easier for her, but he finally admitted that he needed her strength as much as she needed his. It was with surprising pleasure that he decided they made a strong team.

They were nearing the first of the farm buildings, exhausted with the struggle against the wind and cold, when Logan heard the sound of a truck. When the vehicle suddenly appeared in front of them, he shoved Abby to the side, falling after her.

They landed on the hard ground, with her under him. "Abby, are you all right?" he gasped, after yanking down the half muffler.

She blinked several times but didn't speak. He pulled down the wool covering her face and urged her to answer. Her frozen lips barely moved. "I th-think so."

He scarcely hesitated before his lips rubbed over hers, warming with his touch, caressing. His mind went blank as a warmth stole over his entire body. He suddenly didn't care where they were, as long as they were alive—together. He didn't know what would've happened had Floyd not reached them.

"You two okay? What happened? I didn't see you until the last minute. Where's the truck?"

Logan pulled back as Floyd's voice penetrated his mind. He got to his feet, extending a hand to help Abby up beside him. When she was on her feet, he wanted her closer, wrapped in his arms, but she moved toward Floyd.

"Thanks for coming after us."

"Get in the truck. Ellen's been driving me crazy. I can't wait to bring you in."

The heater was going full-blast as they all settled in the cab. Floyd turned the truck around and headed back toward the house. "Hey, you look mighty good in pink, Logan. You making a fashion statement?"

Logan grinned, taking the half muffler in his hand. "Nope, just trying to keep warm. Abby was generous enough to share what she had." He stuffed the hot-pink cloth in his coat pocket. Somehow, it seemed important to hold on to what she had given him.

"Your sister's been mighty impatient, too, pacing the floor. Those two ladies ganged up on me. Now, what happened?" Floyd asked.

"We couldn't get the truck up the backside of the creek," Abby explained.

"Are you half-frozen? That's a long way to walk."

"We made pretty good time," Logan said. "Abby's a strong woman." He couldn't imagine his sister managing to face such a walk.

To his surprise, Abby shifted closer to Floyd. "We're here."

To Logan's surprise, he noted she was right. Floyd had driven the truck right up beside the back porch. He opened the door and got out, then turned to offer Abby a hand. She ignored him and hurried past him into the house.

Now what had he done?

Ellen met Abby at the back door, pulling her into the warmth. "Land's sakes, I was worried about you two. Are you frozen?"

"Almost," Abby muttered as the warm air enveloped her, sending shivers over her body.

"Here's some hot coffee," Lindsay said, holding out a mug.

"Set it on the table. I'm afraid I'd drop it," she said, trying to smile in gratitude. But her skin felt frozen, in spite of the muffler's protection.

Logan and Floyd came inside and received a warm welcome from the two women. They each took the coffee offered and sat down at the table.

Abby didn't sit down. She managed a quick sip and then headed for the stairs. "I'm going to take a hot shower. Thanks again, Floyd, for coming to get us."

"You shouldn't have ever gone out," Lindsay said sternly, the teacherlike tones strange coming from her.

Before Abby could answer, Logan gave his sister a hard stare. "The animals needed to be provided for."

"But you could've been hurt," Lindsay returned, anguish in her voice.

Logan's gaze met Abby's. "No. We knew we could survive. Abby's strong."

His words hurt her again, as they had in the truck. She was strong, not soft and warm, like Lindsay. But she'd obviously been soft enough to kiss. "Yeah, I'm strong…like a man," she said stoically and turned to leave.

"I'll be on my way," Logan said.

She whirled around. "Where are you going?"

"To the bunkhouse. I'd like a shower, too."

"There's no need for you to go outside again. Get more of your clothes from the workroom and shower here. It's only an hour or two before supper." She wouldn't send anyone out in that storm a third time, she told herself. She certainly wasn't being protective of Logan Crawford.

"Yes, Logan, do. Then we can visit after you get warmed up. I've hardly seen you," Lindsay complained, a pout on her lips.

"I had a job to do, Lindsay," he reminded her, but his gaze remained fixed on Abby. "Are you sure, Abby?"

"Of course."

Then she hurried out of the room.

Logan sat down and finished his cup of coffee after Ellen explained there was only one bathroom upstairs. She offered the use of the bath in her and Floyd's apartment, but Logan said he'd wait.

"Abby intended to add another bath or two, but then it turned out she was the only one living up there, so there didn't seem much point," Ellen explained.

"I guess not," he agreed. The sound of the shower being turned on told him Abby was feeling the hot water on her chilled skin. He warmed up considerably thinking about that.

What was wrong with him? If he didn't get his thoughts under control, he was going to do something that would get him fired. When he kissed her, out there in the pasture, their lips had been cold, but he'd felt the heat touching her generated.

He hadn't lost complete control, but he realized it could happen. Under more fortuitous circumstances. Like her naked in the shower.

He cleared his throat. "Abby is a determined woman."

Floyd chuckled. "Surely you're not just figurin' that out? The way I understand it, her aunt Beulah taught her well. That woman has become a legend, running this ranch all by herself."

"Abby?" Lindsay asked.

"No, Beulah Kennedy. Though Abby probably will be, since she takes after her aunt."

"Why didn't her aunt marry, so she'd have a man to take care of everything?" Lindsay asked.

Logan frowned. Was that his sister's answer to problems? Find a man to take care of them? He chastised himself. Wasn't that how she'd been raised?

Until he met Abby, hadn't he believed that was appropriate?

But somehow, after a few days around Abby, Lindsay's attitude seemed...different.

"Mrs. Kennedy was a widow," Ellen said softly. "A one-man woman. She never considered marrying again."

"She probably didn't take time to fix herself up so a man would be interested. Mom says a woman has to be soft and feminine if she's going to catch a man, not smell like cows." Lindsay sleeked back her honey-colored hair, like a cat licks its fur.

"Lindsay, you need to be careful what you say," Logan said sternly, afraid his sister would hurt Abby's feelings. Besides, he was discovering his mother's words didn't hold a lot of truth. Not for him.

Lindsay's gaze widened in surprise. "But it's true, Logan. A wealthy man wants—"

"Enough!" He got up from the table as he heard the shower turn off upstairs. "I'm getting my clothes and going up to take a shower."

He hurried out of the room.

Abby had shampooed her hair while she was in the shower. She'd wanted every inch of her body immersed in the steamy water. But she didn't stay in long. If Logan was going to take a shower, he'd need hot water, too.

Snuggled in a thick terry robe, she combed through her long hair, wishing again it had even a hint of curl. Maybe she had Native American blood in her, because even a hair perm didn't make much difference.

Lindsay's soft curls popped into her mind. The young lady appeared soft everywhere. Soft and feminine. No wonder Logan looked at Abby the way he did, as if he couldn't believe his eyes. No wonder he said she was strong.

"Well, I am," she muttered. And she wasn't going to apologize for it. If she hadn't been strong, the ranch wouldn't be doing so well. If Aunt Beulah hadn't been strong before her, they might not've had a place to live, to be a family.

But the lump in her throat, more than anything else, told her she'd sacrificed to remain strong, in charge. Logan had asked if she didn't want to be a mother. Oh, yes, she wanted children. But more than that, she wanted her own family, her own happiness, a warmth and tenderness that would fill her even during the worst of times.

But it wasn't to be.

Until Logan had come, she'd thought that maybe one day, she'd find a man who would join her, form a family. Then she'd realized that she was an oddity.

A no-man woman.

Strength didn't tempt a man.

Just softness.

She shook herself and lay down the comb. She'd better clear the bath so Logan could have his shower. She'd call down from the top of the stairs on her way to her bedroom.

After quickly creaming her chapped skin, she gathered up her damp towel and dirty clothes and reached around to swing open the bathroom door, only to find Logan poised in front of it, his hand lifted as if to knock.

"Oh!" Abby exclaimed, surprised.

His gaze roamed her face, then focused on her hair.

"I've dreamed of that."

She blinked several times. "Dreamed of what?"

"Seeing your hair loose."

She felt her cheeks heating up and blamed it on the moist warm air in the bathroom. "Sorry I took so long," she hurriedly said and tried to slide past him.

But he didn't move and there wasn't room for both of them through the doorway. Not with his broad shoulders and chest.

"Logan," she began a protest, but when she lifted

her face to look at him, his lips covered hers, as they had in the pasture.

But in the pasture, they'd both been half-frozen. Abby had taken that kiss in stride, figuring it was relief that they'd been rescued.

Rescue wasn't in doubt now. Unless it was rescue from the craziness filling her. Her blood was pumping, her breath shallow, her fingers reaching. They slid through his dark hair as her mouth opened to his.

Suddenly his arms were wrapped around her, his hands stroking her through the robe, pressing her closer. His body was hard against hers. Hard. Strong. Like her.

Memory flooded in her head. He thought she was strong. Like a man. She pulled back, staring at him, looking for something...she didn't know what.

"Abby, I'm sorry," he muttered even as his lips came toward her mouth again.

Oh, yes, he was sorry. He wouldn't want to give her the wrong idea. She pushed against him and slipped through the door. Then she ran down the hall and slammed her door closed behind her.

Damn! Damn! Damn! He'd just made a big mistake.

Kissing Abby had been both heaven and hell. Heaven because the taste of her was even sweeter than he'd hoped it would be. Hell because he figured she'd never let him get close to her again.

If he ever saw her again.

She'd probably send word through Floyd that he should clear out. Especially since his kiss didn't appear to have given her the pleasure he'd experienced.

Pleasure was an inadequate word. He'd shared pleasurable kisses with other women. Abby's kiss was an incredible experience.

Passionate. All-consuming.

One-sided?

He stepped into the bathroom and closed the door as he considered that idea. The moist air, delicately scented with Abby's perfume, enveloped him. No, he was sure she'd been involved, too. He remembered her fingers in his hair, her body pressed against his.

And he didn't remember any resistance until she broke out of his arms.

Encouraged, he stripped and stepped into the hot shower, letting his thoughts, as much as the water, warm him up.

Abby came back downstairs before Logan got out of the shower. She intended to be firmly closeted in her office, doing the hated paperwork, before he emerged to visit with his sister.

When she came into the kitchen, she picked up her coffee mug, still resting on the table, poured out its now cold contents only to pour in more hot coffee. "I'm going to work in my office the rest of the afternoon unless you need any help, Ellen," she said.

"Why, no, Abby," Ellen replied, watching her closely.

Abby wasn't surprised. Ellen hadn't needed any

help with the cooking or taking care of them since she'd moved in over a year ago.

Offering a smile to Ellen, Floyd and Lindsay, she hurried to the kitchen door.

Only to find Lindsay following her into the hallway.

"Abby?"

"Yes, Lindsay?"

"I wondered—well, Ellen and Floyd were explaining about your aunt Beulah."

Abby stared at her. "What about Aunt Beulah?"

"Well, I mean, Logan said—she was alone."

"Yes, she was."

"Well, I don't want to hurt your feelings, but my mother taught me a lot about attracting men, and I wondered if you, you know, wanted me to show you some things to—well, Logan likes pretty women, and—"

As the girl had stumbled around her offer, Abby had grown colder and colder inside. Now she cut her off. "Thanks, anyway, Lindsay, but I imagine it's too late for me to learn those lessons. And if I wanted to learn them, I'd ask my sisters. They've both managed to marry."

"Oh! I'm sorry. I didn't know you had sisters." Lindsay paused and added a brilliant smile. "I wish I had sisters."

Abby reached out and patted Lindsay's shoulder. After all, the girl had only been trying to help. "Thanks, anyway, Lindsay."

"Are you sure, Abby? Logan—"

"I'm sure." She entered her office and closed the

door firmly behind her. She could imagine what Logan had told his sister about her.

It wasn't a pleasant thought.

She tried to work. But thoughts of that moment in the bathroom, caught in Logan's embrace, kept intruding.

What was she going to do now?

She'd promised the man a month's trial, but she couldn't work with him anymore. Not when hunger rose in her every time she thought about him.

"Damn!" she muttered, wiping away the tears that kept trickling down her face. Was it possible she could be falling in love with Logan? And so quickly? And with someone who thought she was strong! Someone who thought she should be soft and feminine, and only found her strong.

She was going to hate that word.

She'd have to ask him to leave.

Coming to that conclusion eased her worries somewhat. She might be attracted to him. Okay, she definitely was attracted to him, but when he was gone, she'd forget. Life would go on as before.

She was sure of it.

The phone rang and she answered. Melissa's voice warmed her.

"Hi, sis. Is everyone okay over there?"

"We're fine. Is Rob in?"

"Yeah, he came in at lunchtime and didn't go out again. I checked with Beth and Jed, too." After a pause, she asked, "I saw a sports car at your place."

"Aha. Now I know the reason for the call. You weren't concerned about me. You just wanted information."

"Abby!" Melissa protested with a chuckle, but she didn't deny the interest in the news.

"It's Logan's sister's car. She drove down to see him."

"Wow. I guess she'll be spending the night."

"Yes, the roads will be too bad to drive on, even if he'd consider letting her drive at night," Abby said, knowing Logan wouldn't.

A beep sounded on the line. "Melissa, I've got another call. I'll talk to you later," Abby promised before she switched lines. "Hello?"

"Miss Kennedy?" a deep voice sounded on the line.

"Yes?"

"This is Caleb Crawford, Logan's father. May I request a favor of you?"

Chapter Nine

Abby stiffened in her chair. "I'll try, Mr. Crawford, if I can."

"Well, my wife and I just discovered that our daughter had invaded your place. We'd appreciate your extending your hospitality to her until we can get down there to pick her up."

Abby breathed a sigh of relief. "We've already invited her to stay tonight, Mr. Crawford. Of course she's welcome. But she has her own vehicle."

"I know that," the man growled, and Abby couldn't hold back a smile at the frustration she heard. He sounded remarkably like his son. "My wife and I wanted to see how Logan was settling in, anyway, but we wouldn't have just barged in without any warning. However, we'll be down as soon as the roads clear to escort that young lady home."

"She's certainly welcome to stay until you arrive.

And you and your wife are welcome to stop over, also.'' If Logan was still there.

Of course he would be there. She couldn't chase him off the ranch in this kind of weather. Her dismissal of the most talented ranch manager she'd ever find would have to wait for the thaw to set in.

And his sister to leave.

And possibly his parents.

She groaned. Probably his mother would offer her lessons on femininity, too, like Lindsay had.

Abby quickly gave directions to the ranch and then hung up with Mr. Crawford.

A soft rap on the door grabbed her attention. ''Yes?'' She silently prayed it wasn't Logan.

Ellen's cheerful face appeared when the door opened. ''Abby? Am I interrupting?''

''No, of course not, Ellen. Is there a problem?''

''Well, Lindsay wanted her brother to spend the night here, with her, well, in a different room, of course, but upstairs, and—''

Abby stared at her. Great. She wanted more distance, and Lindsay was pulling him closer.

''I—I suppose we can do that. Beth's room should be in good shape, if you don't mind fixing the bed and doing a little dusting.''

''It's no trouble at all, as long as you don't mind. That young lady doesn't think much about others,'' Ellen told her, grimacing.

''Is she causing too much work?''

''No, I didn't mean that. She's even offered to help. But…well, she told us what she said to you— I mean, you don't need any lessons, Abby.''

Abby thought she'd experienced enough humiliation today, but it seemed she still had a dose or two coming. Though her cheeks were red, she tried to smile. "Thanks, Ellen, but don't be concerned. She meant well."

"Humph!" Ellen returned and started to back out of the room.

"Oh, Ellen, have you listened to any weather reports?"

"Sure, all day long. They expect the sleet to stop about midnight. Tomorrow, it'll warm up a little and this mess will melt."

"Oh, good. Then Lindsay will be gone tomorrow. Will you still feel up to Sunday night dinner?" It had become a tradition for all the family to dine together on Sunday nights, kind of a chance to catch up on everyone's lives.

"Why, a'course I will. I've already planned the menu."

"Thanks, Ellen."

Abby figured she'd need the normalcy of that event after the past few days. The love she shared with her sisters was a healing balm to the loneliness she sometimes felt.

But she wasn't sure that love would be a quick fix to the pain she was feeling.

Suddenly Logan's head appeared behind Ellen. "Abby? May I speak to you a minute?"

She froze.

Ellen must've seen the panic in her eyes. "Abby has a lot of paperwork."

"Maybe I could help you with it, Abby. I've done some for my dad. We even created a nice computer program to take care of keeping track of the production of calves.''

She wanted to bang her head on the desk. After what happened upstairs, the man wanted to discuss computer programs? It was a good thing she hadn't expected tenderness, caring.

Clearing her throat, she muttered, "No, thanks. I don't need any help. Ellen is going to prepare a room for you, so you and Lindsay will have more time together. Is there anything else?"

He looked at Ellen, then back at Abby. Fortunately, Ellen didn't disappear. Abby reminded herself to give her a bonus. "Uh, yeah. I talked to my parents. I had to let them know where Lindsay was."

Abby pressed her lips together, not looking at the man who was driving her crazy.

"I may have to leave tomorrow to follow her home. Dad doesn't want her out on the road. He's going to call back tomorrow, but when the sleet starts melting—"

"Actually," Abby said with a sigh, "he's already called. He said he and your mother would drive down as soon as the sleet melted. It seems they want to check on you as well as Lindsay."

"Ellen?" Floyd called from the kitchen.

Ellen looked over her shoulder, then back at Abby, indecision on her face.

"I think I'll come get some coffee," Abby said, standing, grabbing her empty mug. If she had to face Logan, she wanted chaperons.

With a frown, Logan stepped back into the hallway to let Ellen and Abby out. As Abby passed him, pressing against the doorjamb to keep as much space as possible between them, he reached out and caught her arm.

"Abby, wait," he whispered and tugged her toward him.

"No!" she whispered and yanked her arm from his hold, rushing after Ellen.

When she reached the kitchen, Floyd was announcing to Ellen that the buzzer went off on the stove.

"Couldn't you take the brownies out of the oven yourself?" Ellen asked in irritation.

Floyd blinked several times, surprise on his face. Abby was pretty sure his beloved Ellen had never talked to him so sharply since their marriage.

"Why, sure, honey, only I didn't know how to tell if they were done. I was afraid I might mess up."

Ellen reached up and kissed his cheek and patted his arm as she moved to the stove. "It's all right."

Which made Abby feel doubly guilty. Poor Floyd shouldn't have to suffer because of her problems. "It's my fault, Floyd. I kept Ellen talking too long."

A quick glance at Logan had her moving toward the coffeepot, which enabled her to keep her back to him.

So she gave a shriek of surprise when she turned around to find him right behind her. Her hand jerked and hot coffee she didn't really want slopped over the side, splashing on the floor and Logan's boots.

Suddenly, everyone in the room crowded around her.

"Dear, did you burn yourself?" Ellen asked, taking the cup from her.

"Sorry," Logan muttered, but he reached for her, not the cup, and Abby pressed back against the counter.

"Damn, boy, you'd better be glad you had your boots on. Here's a towel," Floyd said, surging forward with it.

"What's going on?" Lindsay asked from the door. "Is something wrong?"

"No, I was just being a klutz," Abby said, eager to turn the attention to someone else. She slid along the counter and stepped around Floyd.

She headed for the kitchen door, hoping to escape to her office again, when Logan's voice stopped her. "You forgot your coffee."

"Oh! I—I really don't want any. It—it makes me jittery."

"Do you have to keep working?" Lindsay asked. "I thought maybe we could play a board game or something. Floyd, you and Ellen would like to play Monopoly, wouldn't you?"

Abby almost burst into hysterical laughter at the look on Floyd's face. She didn't think the idea of playing Monopoly had ever crossed Floyd's mind.

Ellen looked at her, as if asking what she wanted them to do. Abby shot a look at Logan. Determination was written all over his face. If she went to her office, he would follow her.

"I think that sounds like a great idea. We've got a couple of hours until dinner, don't we, Ellen? We could all play a game," Abby agreed.

"Oh, goody," Lindsay said with a grin, actually

clapping her hands together. "Our family always used to play games, but they don't do it as much anymore."

"We're all adults, Lindsay," Logan said, exasperation in his voice.

"I'll get the Monopoly game," Abby said, almost running from the room.

"I'll—" Logan began and started moving toward her.

"Logan, could you help me a minute?" Ellen asked, stepping in front of him. "I need someone to hold the pan while I cut the brownies. Then we can have some with our game."

Yes, Ellen definitely deserved a bonus.

Logan watched Abby escape again. He wanted to talk to her in private. They had to clear the air about what had happened. But she clearly didn't want to have that talk. At least not now.

And was being ably assisted by Ellen.

And his sister.

Ever since he'd come down from his shower, Lindsay had claimed all his attention. Including calling his father. Then, before he could get to Abby, his father had called her. He must've said something to upset her.

Or she was upset about what had happened upstairs.

By the time Abby returned with the game, Ellen had finished cutting the brownies. Then she asked him to hold the plate while she put the brownies on it. He knew the cabinet would do a better job, since he jerked around every time he thought he heard the door open. But his mother wouldn't forgive him if he didn't honor a lady's request.

Abby and Lindsay came back in together, laughing.

He hadn't seen Abby laugh before. Her eyes sparkled and she was more relaxed than he'd ever seen her. The urge to press his lips against her smile had him moving in her direction with the brownie plate still clutched in his hands.

"Hey, boy, where you going with the brownies?" Floyd called, awakening Logan from his trance.

"Uh, yeah, to the table. Right, Ellen?"

"Yes, dear," Ellen said and patted him on the shoulder.

Feeling like a little boy who'd stubbed his toe in front of the entire school, Logan set the plate on the table and moved around it toward Abby.

She immediately turned in the other direction and began helping Floyd carry glasses of lemonade to the table.

"Sit here by me, Logan," Lindsay demanded, clutching his arm.

With a sigh, he sat by his sister. Abby immediately chose the seat at the head of the table, as far from him as possible. Big surprise.

Two hours later, he'd gotten no closer to Abby. She'd held her own at the end of the table, amassing a pretend fortune. Floyd, who'd gotten into the spirit of the game, was doing well, too. Ellen had checked out early, which made it possible for her to fix supper while they continued the game.

Logan landed on one of Abby's hotels.

"That does it for me," he said, throwing the fake

money he had, a pitifully small amount, on the board. "You've wiped me out, Abby."

Rather than look at him, she muttered, "Someone has to win," and concentrated on gathering what money he'd had.

"You get to collect the rest from the bank," Lindsay assured her. When she'd had to drop out, she'd become the banker.

"Thanks, but I think we'd better put everything away. Dinner's almost ready, right, Ellen?" Then, before she could stop herself, she sneezed.

Logan leaped to his feet. "You caught a cold!"

"Oh, dear!" Ellen exclaimed, moving over to lay her hand on Abby's forehead.

"Please," Abby protested. "I sneezed. It's not the end of the world."

"I think you feel a little warm," Ellen said, her hand moving to Abby's cheek.

Logan stared, wishing he could touch her, too.

"I'm fine. But just to be sure, I'll take a couple of pills. But you know I'm never sick, Ellen."

"That's what you thought about Melissa, too, and she got mononucleosis."

"The kissing disease?" Lindsay asked in surprise. She turned to Abby. "Who have you been kissing, Abby?" she teased.

Logan hid his groan, his gaze fastened on Abby's flushed cheeks.

Ellen immediately spoke. "Don't be silly, Lindsay. That may be its nickname, but the disease is passed around like a cold, I think. Which means you'd better keep your distance from Abby until we figure out what she has."

Abby jumped up from the table and began backing toward the door. "That's right. I'd better stay in my room the rest of the evening. I don't want to make anyone else sick."

"I'll bring you a tray, dear, after I serve dinner to the men."

"Thanks, Ellen. I'd better—" she broke off and sneezed again. "Oh. I'll—I'll go to bed."

And she disappeared up the stairs.

"Floyd," Ellen said, "you'd better ring the dinner bell. I'm sure the men are hungry."

Lindsay stared at Ellen. "You mean the men take *all* their meals here? With the family?"

This time Logan didn't hide his groan. Grabbing his sister by her shoulders, he pulled her out of the kitchen, sending Ellen and Floyd an apologetic smile over his shoulder.

"Little sister, you've put your foot in your mouth one too many times," he informed her when they reached the hallway.

Abby was bored.

She'd been relieved for the excuse to avoid Logan. She figured it was the tension she was experiencing as much as the cold that brought on her sneezing. Psychosomatic.

Or something like that.

But after trying to read a book, some murder mystery that Beth had given her, and finding it impossible to stay focused on the written word, she'd put the book aside.

Now she lay against the pillows piled up behind her and stared at the four walls.

She'd hoped she'd get away from Logan by hiding. But she'd discovered that thought of him remained with her. Thoughts of his touch, his words, his masculine presence.

Had Aunt Beulah felt like this about her husband? Abby had once asked her why she hadn't remarried. The woman had gotten a gentle smile on her face and murmured, "No one else ever touched my heart."

Ellen always said Beulah was a one-man woman. Abby wondered if she could have that same problem. Because she was pretty sure Logan Crawford had touched her heart. And other parts as well.

And she wanted more.

She gave a gusty sigh. She'd die a virgin if that was true. Of course, she could offer herself to Logan, hoping he'd be interested enough to take her to bed, even if he'd never marry her. From his kiss, she'd guess there was some interest.

The only other time she'd contemplated going to bed with a man had been when she'd been taking a couple of courses at Midwestern State in Wichita Falls. She'd had a discussion with Aunt Beulah about sex and had ultimately decided she wouldn't have sex with the man she was attracted to until there was some kind of commitment.

After she told the guy her decision, he told her she wasn't pretty enough anyway.

Pretty, feminine, soft.

She was strong.

Another sigh slipped through her pressed lips.

Someone knocked on her bedroom door.

Abby frowned. Only Ellen would be asking to come in, surely. Cautiously she called, "Who is it?"

After a hesitation, Logan answered, "It's me. I need to talk to you, Abby."

She checked her watch. "It's almost ten."

"I won't take long."

"I—I don't feel well," she pleaded. So much for being strong.

"I just wanted to apologize."

She knew what for. He'd already said he was sorry once. "It doesn't matter."

"Yes, it does. Lindsay shouldn't have—"

Abby bolted up in bed. "Lindsay? What does it have to do with Lindsay?"

The door opened and Logan slipped into the room. Abby grabbed the covers and pulled them up to her chin, as if they'd offer protection from the man's potent attraction.

"What did you think I was talking about?"

Her red cheeks probably told him more than words.

"I'm not apologizing for kissing you, Abby," he said roughly.

"You already did," she reminded him.

He stepped closer to the bed, a rueful grin on his face. "Yeah, but I didn't mean it."

"Then why did you—"

"You seemed startled, upset."

"I'm your boss," she reminded him, her chin rising. "That was inappropriate behavior."

"So I can't kiss you again until you're not my boss?" His gaze had narrowed to her lips.

Her breathing shortened, and she seemed to be

gasping for air. Especially when she realized he would no longer be working for her as soon as his family had left. But then he'd be gone, too.

"Uh, yes."

He stared at her and took another step closer, making her nervous.

"What did you want to say about Lindsay? If you're apologizing for her spending the night, don't be ridiculous. You know ranchers are hospitable."

"No, I wouldn't apologize for that again. But when she offered to teach you how to attract men, she was way off base."

"How did you know?" she blurted out.

"I was chewing her out for another inappropriate remark when she decided to confess. Lindsay's honest if nothing else."

"She's a charming young woman, soft and feminine. I knew she was only trying to help."

"You don't need any help in the attraction area, Abby. You should know that." He continued to stare at her lips. "Our little session in the bathroom should've convinced you of that."

"Men don't—don't find me attractive!" she snapped, wanting him to go away before she melted in humiliation.

"You've got to be kidding!" Logan grinned, as if she'd just told a funny joke.

"No, I'm not," she returned, angry that he was laughing at her. "Someone told me."

"A jealous woman? You wouldn't—"

"A man! A man I—I cared about." Then she wished she'd kept her mouth shut. What was that saying about better to keep silent than to confirm your stupidity with your own words?

He reached the bed and sat on the side of it, way too close to her, in Abby's opinion. "Tell me."

"No! It's my business and none of yours."

He kept staring at her, his gaze compelling. "Tell me, Abby."

He obviously didn't believe her, thought she was making up the story. "Fine. We'd dated and he— he wanted to have sex. I said no, and he said it didn't matter anyway. I wasn't pretty enough to interest him."

Logan stared at her. Then he burst into laughter.

Abby came off the bed swinging, anger surging through her. She thought she might've landed a blow or two, from the stinging on her hands, before Logan hauled her against him and buried his face against her neck.

"Turn me loose! How dare you laugh at me!"

"Sweetheart, you don't know a blasted thing about men, do you?" He pulled back, still grinning at her.

"Of course I do! I work with them every day."

Instead of answering, his lips covered hers and the magic she'd found earlier in his arms returned full-force. She got that strange tingling over her whole body again and the world seemed to stop turning on its axis. But she knew better than to give in. Wrenching her face to one side, she tried to wriggle out of his arms.

"Abby, the reason the guy said that is because you wounded his ego," Logan said gently.

"You don't know—"

"Yes, I do. If he didn't want you, why was he trying to get you in bed?"

"Because—because no one else was available?" she asked, the logic of his words slowing her down.

He slowly shook his head.

"But—but I'm not feminine...."

Logan lifted a hand and smoothed back a strand of hair that had escaped from her braid. "Don't be silly. I've never met a more feminine woman."

"You're—you're just saying that because you want to get in my bed!" she protested, afraid to believe the tenderness she heard in his voice.

He leaned toward her and Abby knew he was going to kiss her again. This time she wanted him to touch her, to let her experience the magic, the—

A knock sounded on the door.

"Another time," Logan promised.

Chapter Ten

The door opened and Ellen said, "Abby, dear, did you need— Oh!"

"No! No, don't go, Ellen," Abby said as the older woman began retreating. "Logan was just leaving." She stared at the man whose arms were still around her.

He stood, reluctantly it seemed to Abby, and cleared his throat. "Uh, yeah, I, uh, just had something I needed to clear up with Abby." He moved over to the door, but before he left the room, he turned to stare at her again. "Think about what I've said, Abby."

Then he disappeared again.

"Are you all right, dear? You know Floyd would protect you if—"

Abby gave a tremulous smile. "I'm fine, Ellen. And I know I can count on you and Floyd. Everything's fine."

"Then I'll say good night," Ellen said with a gentle smile and turned to go.

"Ellen—" Abby called, then stopped in embarrassment.

"Yes, dear?" Ellen asked, facing her again. "Do you need some more pills? Or water?"

"No. But, Ellen, do you think I'm feminine?"

Ellen shook her head and Abby's heart sank. So much for Logan's kind words.

"That's the most ridiculous question I've ever heard you ask, Abby Kennedy."

Hope sprang up immediately. "It is? I'm not pretty, like my sisters. I work like a man. I—"

"You're a strong woman."

That hated word!

"But that doesn't make you any less of a woman. Some men wouldn't be strong enough to hold their own. You'd scare them. But for the right man, Abby Kennedy, you'd be the most feminine woman in the world."

"Aunt Beulah said I should stay away from men," Abby said, frowning.

Ellen came over to the bed and leaned down to kiss Abby's forehead. "Your aunt had already had her romance. She was trying to protect you. But she was wrong. If you don't risk your heart, you can't win."

Then Ellen tiptoed from the room, leaving Abby to think about the events of the day.

Logan thumped the pillow again. He wished he was in the bunkhouse. Not that the bed wasn't comfortable. It was. But it was too near Abby's room.

The temptation of knowing the woman he wanted was only a few feet away was killing him. He couldn't return to her room. That wouldn't be right.

He'd already gone too far when he'd knocked on her door earlier. But he'd had to clear the air about Lindsay. Damn his little sister. If Abby were any more attractive to him, he'd throw her over his shoulder and play caveman.

And if her kisses were anything to go by, she'd meet him more than halfway. After all, she wasn't a child. And she was as attracted to him as he was to her. He was sure of it.

After his sister left, he'd get more time with Abby, and he intended an all-out assault. He wasn't going to let her hide behind that jerk's stupid words. If the man believed that, he had no taste in women.

Thank God Abby hadn't fallen for his line.

Logan hated the thought of her giving herself to some jerk who didn't know how to appreciate her.

In fact, he hated the thought of her giving herself to anyone but himself. But he couldn't expect a woman twenty-eight years old to be untried, just as she couldn't expect—

Suddenly he froze. Word by word, he went back over Abby's statements. She'd never talked about having sex with anyone. She said she'd refused.

Hell, was she a virgin?

That thought paralyzed him. Both fear and wonder welled up in him. Abby had never…he was positive of it now. Which meant he'd need to exercise care when he touched her. He mustn't frighten her. He'd have to be sure she understood what she was doing.

He'd have to *not* seduce her.

Damn! His body was revved up, eager to be with her, to claim her as his, and he couldn't. Unless—

Was he ready for marriage?

He'd avoided even the idea of marriage in all his past relationships. *Because he'd been bored.* That thought had never occurred to him before. But women, in the past, had been a peripheral thing, something for pleasure. Not an integral part of his life.

Abby had been central from day one.

His day began and ended with time spent with Abby.

A grin spread across his face and he tucked his hands behind his head. Just thinking about days spent at Abby's side, nights spent the same way, excited him more than anything had since he'd gotten his first pony when he was six.

A chuckle rippled through him. Somehow, he wasn't sure she'd appreciate his analogy. But he'd make her understand. He'd considered a woman to be a burden, something, someone to protect, care for, but with Abby it was different. Just as they'd struggled together in the storm, so would they face life, together, combining their strengths to do even more than either could do alone.

Matching their best assets in their children.

He immediately pictured a little girl with long braids, running to meet him as he came home. Or a son, riding his first pony.

Or Abby, her stomach rounded with their child.

He groaned and buried his face in the pillow

again. Much more daydreaming like that and he'd have to take another shower. This one ice-cold.

When Abby awoke the next morning, she discovered the only remnant of her supposed cold was a small case of the sniffles. But she didn't hurry from her bed.

It was Sunday morning. The few chores that had to be done were rotated among her and the men, so that most everyone had this one day free. Even Ellen wasn't required to provide meals for the men on Sundays.

Even with the thought, Abby smelled the scent of bacon drifting up the stairs. Ellen might not cook for Dirk and Barney, but she always cooked for Abby and Floyd. And this morning, Abby knew she would cook for Logan and Lindsay, too.

Ellen wasn't going to get much time off.

Since she was so wide-awake, Abby decided she might as well dress and go to the kitchen. She wasn't one to lie in bed all morning.

A sudden flash of Logan leaning over her last night had her shutting down any thoughts about sharing her bed, perhaps finding a reason to linger there. She moved even faster than ever, anxious to exit the bedroom.

The kitchen, with other people, would be less conducive to flights of fantasy. And it was fantasy. Because she'd already made up her mind to dismiss Logan. As soon as his family was gone.

She brushed and braided her hair in her traditional one long braid. Not bothering with makeup, she hurried down the stairs, only to find Logan, Ellen and Floyd sitting at the table.

"Good morning. Where's Lindsay?"

"I'm afraid my sister's not an early riser," Logan said even as his gaze roved her face and body. "How are you feeling this morning?"

"Fine. False alarm, I guess," she said briskly, avoiding his eyes. To give herself something to do, she took down a mug and filled it at the coffeepot.

"Better eat a good breakfast to keep you healthy," Ellen said as she joined them at the table where there was a clean place setting. "There's plenty of eggs and bacon and biscuits."

She filled her plate and looked up to discover all three of them watching her. "I have a good appetite," she said stiffly, thinking they were criticizing how much she was eating.

"'Course you do," Floyd said. "And you work hard, too."

"It's a sign you're not sick," Ellen added.

Logan just grinned.

She wanted to punch his lights out. Namby-pamby females in books could never eat when they were with a man they adored. But Abby wasn't a namby-pamby female. She squared her jaw and stared back at him.

Instead of referring to her breakfast, Logan said, "We heard a weather forecast. Most of the sleet has stopped. It should start melting today, so I reckon we can clear that herd out of the south pasture."

Okay, they'd talk business. "Good. I'll need to pull the truck out of the creek this afternoon. The water level might rise with the sleet melting."

"Floyd and I can do that," Logan said.

"*I* can do—"

"I know you can, Abby, but why risk making your cold worse when there's no need?"

"That makes sense, Abby," Ellen pointed out quietly.

"I don't have a cold," she protested and then ruined it all by sneezing again. "That's the first time I've sneezed this morning!"

Logan ducked his head and took a bite of his scrambled eggs.

In fact, no one said anything for several minutes. Then Floyd stood. "Well, I'd best get to the chores."

"Is it your Sunday, Floyd?" Abby asked, surprised.

"Yep, it is."

"I'll help you," Logan said, rising to his feet.

"No need, Logan. We got a system," Floyd said.

"Good, you can explain it to me as we work."

The two men walked out of the kitchen, in perfect agreement.

"Why did Floyd let him get away with that?" Abby demanded when she found her voice.

"Probably because he'll get out of the cold a lot faster," Ellen informed her with a smile. "I like that man. He doesn't run away from work."

"No. No, he's a good man." And she was going to fire him. She'd promised herself.

"I'm going to get some of that miserable paperwork done while they're gone. After all, if Lindsay has her way, we'll be playing more games later."

"Won't she be going home this afternoon?"

"I don't know. Her parents said they were coming down to take her home."

"But she's got her own car."

"The Crawfords are a very protective family."

Ellen shook her head. "I'm not sure that's a good thing. I mean, Beulah taught you girls to be tough. It didn't hurt you, and you manage just fine on your own."

"I know," Abby said, smiling as she thought of her aunt. "But Lindsay is...is very appealing."

Ellen sniffed and began clearing the table.

Logan and Floyd worked side by side, cleaning the stalls in the barn, feeding the animals there. When they'd completed all those chores, Floyd muttered, "Might be best to pull the truck out now, before we go back to the house. That way Abby can't argue about it."

"Good thinking, Floyd," Logan agreed, pleased with his idea. "You want to drive the tractor?"

"Yeah. You ride with me, then drive the truck back once we get it out."

The two men bundled up and set about doing the chore. While it was still cold, sleet was no longer falling and the wind had died down somewhat.

Logan had decided, after greeting Abby this morning, that the more distance he put between the two of them this morning, the better off things would be. While he may have discovered feelings for Abby, he was pretty sure she didn't feel the same way.

If she did, she'd at least look at him.

Besides, he'd only been on the ranch four days.

He could afford to give her more time to get used to him before they explored their attraction. As long as he didn't get too close. When he was within touching distance, he found her hard to resist.

"How long have you and Ellen been here, Floyd?" he asked the older man as they worked.

"Jed brought me here right after he came to train Beth. Then Ellen moved in a few weeks later."

"You didn't come together?" Logan had assumed they'd come as a married couple.

"Nope. Ellen was a neighbor of the girls, a widow. I got lucky when I met her. I mean, meeting her was lucky," Floyd exclaimed. "I didn't mean—"

Logan laughed. "I understand." And he understood what the other man was trying to say. Logan felt lucky that he'd come to the Circle K when he did. Before another man discovered Abby Kennedy.

"It's a good place to work," Floyd added. "Abby's a special lady."

"Very special."

"I wasn't sure you realized that when you first came."

Logan eyed the other cowboy. "Abby's a lot different from the women in my family. But I'm a fast learner."

"Just don't keep telling her she shouldn't work," Floyd warned.

"No, I won't. But I've only got a month. I'm here on a trial basis only," he warned. "Abby could decide to send me on my way then."

"Not if you play it smart. But Ellen told me—I

mean, Abby's a shy lady. You can't push her too fast.''

Logan raised one eyebrow but said nothing.

Floyd added, his voice growing stern, ''And anybody who takes advantage of her will have to fight me.''

Floyd was only confirming what Logan had already figured out. He'd been rushing his fences. Best to slow down and woo Abby properly. If he could.

''I won't hurt her, Floyd.''

The other man nodded and went back to fastening the chains on the front bumper of the truck.

Lindsay joined Abby and Ellen in the kitchen midmorning when they were taking a coffee break.

''Sorry I slept so long,'' she said with a winsome smile. ''Mom's always complaining about my sleeping in, but I don't do it all that often.''

''No problem,'' Abby said. ''Coffee's fresh if you want a cup.''

''I'll cook you some breakfast, too, if you'll tell me what you'd like,'' Ellen offered.

''Oh, I'll fix me a piece of toast to go with the coffee. That will be plenty,'' Lindsay assured her.

When she was seated at the table, Lindsay asked, ''Where's Logan?''

''He's helping Floyd with the chores,'' Ellen said.

''Logan's a hard worker,'' Lindsay said, before adding, ''All my brothers are. They take after my dad. Mom works hard, too, but in different ways.''

Abby managed a pleasant smile but said nothing. She wasn't learning anything new.

Lindsay giggled. ''Mom's been working on getting a touring company from the New York City Ballet to give a performance in Lawton. That's the biggest town near us.''

Ellen stared at the girl. "Ballet? You think anyone would go?"

"Oh, yes. Mom has promised it will sell out if they'll come. They're doing a one-night performance in Oklahoma City and Mom got the idea of bringing them to Lawton. She's worked tirelessly to bring it off. The proceeds will go to support the women's shelter.''

"How nice," Abby said.

"That's not what Dad and my brothers said. They don't want to go, but they know they'll have to.''

Abby had a mental image of Logan in a tuxedo, attending the ballet with some beautiful woman in an evening gown. She couldn't imagine herself in such a situation, but she could see Logan there.

"I'm sure that will be the social event of the year," Ellen said, a touch of dryness in her voice.

"Hey, I could get tickets for you," Lindsay said, smiling eagerly.

"Thanks, but I don't think we'll be able to attend," Abby said firmly.

"Well, there's always the Christmas Ball. That's another of Mom's projects. And the Spring Festival. She's copying the Oklahoma City Arts Festival. Have you ever been there? There's a square downtown and artists display their work for everyone to look at. There are food vendors and a local radio show broadcasts from there. You can buy all kinds of things.''

Nothing could have pointed out to Abby how different she was from Logan's family. She'd scarcely been beyond Wichita Falls. Dreams of foreign travel may have filled her head when she was younger, but there'd been no time. Though running the ranch was her dream, she'd also hoped to find a reliable manager and take a trip or two in the future.

But the ballet, a Christmas Ball or a Spring Festival was beyond the scope of her life. She was sure Mrs. Crawford's efforts would enrich many lives, but it only pointed out their differences.

She picked up her coffee mug and stood. "We're going to have sandwiches at lunch because Ellen will be cooking a big meal for this evening. I hope that's all right with you."

Lindsay grinned. "I'd love to have sandwiches. Mom always insists on a big meal."

"Yes, I'm sure she does," Abby said and hurried from the kitchen. She didn't want to hear any more about the Crawfords.

As the weather improved, Logan and Floyd decided to move the herd from the south pasture. From the barn, Floyd called Barney and Dirk and asked if they'd mind helping. Then he called Ellen and asked for some sandwiches he and Logan could eat while they worked.

In no time, they had everything organized, all without Abby being involved.

"She's going to be angry, isn't she?" Logan asked.

"Probably not. Once it's done, she moves on. She's not one to hold a grudge," Floyd assured him.

"'Sides," Barney added as they rode out to the

south pasture. "She deserves a day off. She works too hard."

Logan could agree with that.

With all four men working, they accomplished their task in a couple of hours and were back at the barn by three o'clock. When the horses had been taken care of, Logan thanked the other men and he and Floyd headed toward the house.

They were almost there, when a Lincoln TownCar pulled up near the house.

"Guests?" Floyd guessed, rubbing his chin as he studied the new arrivals.

Logan suppressed a grin. "Not exactly. My parents, come to corral their girlchild." He strode over to receive his mother's hug and kiss on the cheek.

His father gave him a bear hug that surprised him. He said, "Hi, Dad. Good to see you."

"You, too, son."

"Are you eating well?" his mother asked. "You look like you've lost weight."

Logan shook his head. "Mom, I've only been gone four days. And Ellen is the best cook in Texas. Here's Floyd, her husband and one of the crew," he added, waving Floyd over. "Floyd, this is my mother, Carol, and my father, Caleb Crawford."

Greetings were exchanged. Then Floyd invited them into the house where he assured them Ellen would have a pot of coffee on.

"I thought Miss Kennedy's name was Abigail," his mother said with a frown.

"It is. Ellen is her housekeeper," Logan said.

"Oh, of course. It's very smart of her to have help

so she has time for more important things,'' Carol said, nodding in approval.

Logan bit down on his bottom lip. He wanted to urge his mother to not hurt Abby's feelings, fearful she, like his sister, would be critical of Abby's lifestyle. But he couldn't in front of Floyd.

Floyd was right about coffee being available. Ellen greeted everyone at the door, then offered the brew, which was heartily accepted by Caleb.

As soon as everyone was seated at the kitchen table, Ellen excused herself to go find Abby and Lindsay.

"I'm sure Miss Kennedy is relieved to have such a competent manager as you, Logan. It must be a real relief for her," Carol said, proud of her son.

Logan looked at Floyd, figuring the man would speak up in Abby's defense, but he said nothing.

"Abby knows the ranching business, Mom. The ranch is in great shape."

"It looks like it," Caleb said. "I saw a herd on the way in. They're in good condition."

Abby came to the kitchen, dressed as usual in her jeans and shirt, followed by Lindsay in tailored pants and a sweater. It appeared his sister had come with a full wardrobe.

Introductions were made and the two ladies joined the others at the table. Caleb Crawford congratulated Abby on how well-run her ranch appeared and asked several questions about her operation. Carol protested, pointing out that it was Sunday, not a workday, though she eyed Abby's attire with a questioning look.

Logan watched Abby as she smiled politely. Then

she looked at him. "You and Floyd were gone a long time."

He heard the question, but his mother stepped in before he could respond. "Surely Sunday is Logan's free time."

Abby stiffened and he hurried to answer. "We retrieved the truck and moved the herd."

Abby's gaze widened, then narrowed. "I don't believe I asked you to do that."

Several voices responded in an attempt to satisfy the anger in her voice. Caleb asked about the truck and its need to be retrieved. Floyd tried to take responsibility for their actions. Carol Crawford protested her son's work on a Sunday.

Logan said nothing, but he stared at Abby, willing her to leave the questions until his parents had departed. And he hoped they left soon.

The phone grabbed Abby's attention. Everyone quieted as Abby answered. It became obvious that something was wrong as she tensed and her cheeks grew pale.

Logan leaped from his chair to stand beside her, watching her face.

"What's wrong?" Ellen demanded as Abby hung up the phone.

"I've got to go!" Abby exclaimed, turning toward the door.

Logan grabbed her arm. "Tell us what's wrong first and what we can do to help."

"Beth just went into labor!"

Chapter Eleven

"**S**he's not even seven months yet," Abby explained. "Jed's taking her to the hospital in Tumbleweed, but they may transfer her to Wichita Falls. Melissa and I are going to meet them there."

"I'll come, too," Ellen exclaimed, as upset as Abby. Then she looked at her husband. "Oh, I can't. I haven't cooked dinner yet."

"Don't you worry about nothing," Floyd assured her. "We'll manage."

Abby had already run from the room. Ellen followed her.

"Who is Beth?" Lindsay asked.

"Abby's youngest sister." He looked at his father. "Her husband is Jed Davis."

His father blinked in surprise. "Is that right? He's a good man. They live near here?"

"Just across the road."

Abby came rushing back through the kitchen, her coat on. "I'm sorry to leave but—"

"Don't worry about it," Logan assured her, lifting one hand to caress her pale cheek. "Drive carefully and let us know what's happening when you can."

"The ranch—"

"I'll take care of everything. You be with Beth."

Relief poured over her features, making Logan feel that he'd helped her. A good feeling. "Thank you, Logan."

Ellen joined her and, after giving Floyd a quick kiss, she and Abby hurried from the house.

"I don't like her driving when she's so upset," Logan said, thinking about what he could do.

"Maybe Rob will drive them," Floyd suggested.

"And leave all the kids alone?"

"Children? We could help care for the children," Carol suggested.

Logan grabbed the phone. He caught Melissa as she was leaving the house. When he explained that they'd care for the children if Rob wanted to go with them, Melissa immediately accepted the offer.

"We'll be right over, Melissa. You two go ahead with Abby and Ellen."

In five minutes, everyone's plans for the rest of the day changed dramatically. Carol and Lindsay immediately went to Melissa's house, with Logan to perform the introductions, to take care of the six children, though Wayne and Terri both thought they were old enough to manage without any adults.

Carol Crawford might be ignorant about ranching, though Logan wasn't sure about his mother's lack of knowledge, but she knew children. With great skill, she managed to make the two older children feel valued while she took charge of the household.

Then she ordered Logan to go take care of ranch business, ignoring the fact that it was Sunday and she'd protested his earlier working. She added that her husband, son and Floyd should come to Melissa's house for dinner that evening.

Logan stomped back to Abby's house, growling to himself. "Like we can't even fend for ourselves for one evening."

He complained to his father and Floyd when he got back to the kitchen.

Caleb grinned. "That's your mother. She can be bossy, but she's mighty handy in a crisis."

"Yeah," Logan agreed with a sigh. He was glad to know Rob was with the women. And he didn't have to worry about his mom offending Abby, either. But he hoped and prayed Beth and the baby would be all right.

"Now let's talk about the little lady who just ran out of here," Caleb said, motioning for his son to be seated.

Logan looked at him warily. He was pretty sure his father didn't mean Ellen. So he must've revealed his feelings somehow.

Floyd grinned. "You'll want to be private. I'll go down to the bunkhouse and tell the guys about Beth. We're all family here, and they'll want to know."

When Floyd had disappeared, Logan stalled by filling his cup with more coffee. He raised the coffeepot in a silent question to his father, but he shook his head.

"Nice lady, Abby Kennedy," Caleb said.

"Yeah."

"Young. I thought the owner was old."

"That was Beulah Kennedy, her aunt. She died about two years ago."

"Ah," Caleb said. After a silence, he asked, "Who's been managing the ranch?"

"Abby. Rob managed it briefly until he got too busy with a rodeo supply company they started. But Abby's managed it for seven or eight years now, since her aunt got too old."

"She must be good."

Logan nodded. His father had more questions, he knew.

"It's tough to mix business and pleasure."

Logan cleared his throat. But he couldn't think of anything to say, so he nodded in agreement.

"Is that going to be a problem?"

"Maybe," Logan admitted. "I—I've only been here a few days, but Abby... She's different from any woman I've ever known."

Caleb nodded, a pleased look in his eye. "Good ranching stock."

"She's not like Mom. Abby's a great hand, a hard worker, knows ranching backward and forward. She doesn't do charity work, or any of that social stuff."

Caleb grinned. "No problem. You'll have a lot in common."

Logan sat back in relief. "Yeah. Now all I have to do is convince Abby of that."

They transferred Beth to Wichita Falls under the care of a specialist. Abby had already called the ranch once to let them know that none of them would be returning tonight. Melissa had talked to her kids. Ellen had talked to Floyd.

Once Beth was settled in her room, the labor pains having stopped, Jed by her side, Rob insisted he, Melissa, Abby and Ellen get two rooms for the night at the hotel across the street from the hospital.

When she and Ellen, with toothbrushes and other items purchased in the gift shop, closed the door to their room, Abby immediately went to the phone. It was already after ten, but she needed to talk to…to Logan.

It amazed her, even scared her, at how much she was relying on the man.

When he answered the phone in the house, she wasn't surprised.

"Logan?"

"Abby, is Beth all right? And you?"

"Beth is doing fine. They've stopped the pains. And of course I'm all right."

"Of course," he said with a soft chuckle that caressed her soul.

"I wanted to let you know we're in the Meridian Hotel next to the hospital. I haven't thought about what needs to be done tomorrow but—"

"Floyd and I have worked everything out. Don't worry about the ranch. We'll take care of things."

"Oh, Logan, I appreciate it so much. I know I kind of left everything hanging, but—"

"Abby, it was an emergency," he reminded her gently.

"Yes. Your parents?"

"Are still here. Dad and Mom are staying at Melissa's to take care of the kids."

"Your mother? But—"

"She's loving it, having six kids to boss around again. And Lindsay is helping her."

"I'm sure we'll be back sometime tomorrow. Once she gets the kids off to school, if you can spare Barney or Floyd, they can watch the little ones until we—"

"We'll manage. Just take care of yourself, okay?"

"Logan, I'm not in any danger," Abby protested, but to herself she admitted that his concern for her was warming.

"I know, but...we miss you."

Abby didn't know how to respond, though her heart cried out with the urge to reply in kind. "Thank you for helping out."

"No problem. Take care now. And Floyd is waiting to talk to Ellen."

"Bye," Abby said softly and handed the phone to her roommate.

She took a quick shower while Ellen talked, giving her a little privacy. When she opened the door to the bedroom again, Ellen had the television on, but her eyes were suspiciously red.

"Ellen, is everything all right? The hospital didn't call?"

"No! No, everything's fine. I'm just a silly old woman."

"No, you're not. Why did you cry?"

Ellen gave her a rueful smile. "Lots of reasons. Relief that Beth and the baby will be all right. Missing Floyd. This is our first night apart since we got married. And gratitude that I'm part of this family."

"Of course you're part of this family," Abby exclaimed. Since Ellen had moved in with them, she'd become a surrogate grandmother to Melissa's children, and a mother figure to Abby and her sisters.

Ellen sniffed. "You know, two years ago, I was all alone and thought the best years of my life were over. Now, my life is so full of joy."

The two women hugged before Ellen briskly suggested Abby go on to bed while she showered. "We'll want to be up early to check on Beth in the morning," she added.

With a weary smile, Abby agreed. When Ellen closed the bathroom door, leaving the bedroom in darkness, Abby gave thanks for Beth's recovery. Then she closed her eyes and immediately thought of Logan.

Maybe, if she could keep her distance from him, maybe she wouldn't have to fire Logan. He was so reliable, so trustworthy, so...strong. Maybe she could leave him in charge and do some traveling, as she'd planned.

Somehow, the appeal for travel was gone.

She certainly couldn't leave before roundup next week. And she couldn't leave until after Beth's baby was safely delivered. And there was Christmas with the family. Then spring would bring calving season. And the spring roundup.

As sleep overcame, she pictured her and Logan, dealing with the day-to-day life on a ranch, discussing—no, that wasn't right. Logan didn't want to discuss ranch life with her. But somehow, in her dreams, that didn't matter.

Melissa rapped on their door at seven the next morning.

Abby was surprised to find herself still in bed. She'd thought she and Ellen would both be awake earlier, as was their norm.

Melissa dismissed their apologies. "Don't be silly. We all had a stressful day yesterday. Jed is showering in our room. The doctor has already been in this morning and Beth and the baby are doing fine. He wants to keep her another night to be sure. Then she can go home."

"Really? Just like that?" Abby demanded. "But what caused it?"

"They're not sure. And she gets to go home, but she's to stay in bed most of the time," Melissa added. "It's a good thing they hired Clara," she said, naming the housekeeper Jed had insisted on hiring once they discovered Beth was pregnant.

Abby frowned. "I hope Beth will follow the doctor's orders."

"She will," Melissa assured her. "Beth may be hardheaded, but she won't risk the baby's health."

"That's right," Ellen agreed. "And we'll find ways to keep her from getting bored."

A feeling of a family united satisfied Abby deep within. "How's Jed holding up?"

"Pretty well. Rob's been making a list of things to do on his place. He'll stay here until Beth goes home, but Rob thought we might go on home today."

Ellen nodded eagerly. "As long as Beth doesn't need us."

Melissa agreed. "We'll have breakfast together as soon as Jed's ready. Then we'll go see Beth. After that, maybe we'll go home."

Those words echoed in Abby's heart. Go home. As long as Beth didn't need them, they could go home. Logan's face flashed in her head with those words, but she worked at dismissing it. Of course, he had nothing to do with going home. He'd only been there four days, five if you counted today.

But if he stayed, she'd have more freedom.

That was why she thought of him. Of course.

Logan started the roundup the next morning.

With Floyd's assistance, he called several of the ranchers in the area and borrowed three more hands, with promises to repay the loan when the ranchers conducted their own roundups. With Jed, Rob and Abby gone, they needed more help.

The first day went smoothly, and Logan figured they'd finish in three more days. His father, having accompanied him, agreed.

"This is a very nice operation," Caleb said again as they rode back to the house. "Think the lady would want to sell?"

Logan jerked his head around to stare at his father. "Sell? Abby would never sell. Besides, I told you I—I hope—"

"I know what you told me. But a man needs to have the upper hand. You don't want to marry the boss. You want to *be* the boss."

Logan frowned. He didn't agree with his father

about having to be the boss. He wanted to be partners with his wife, sharing everything. And Abby was the first woman he'd met who was strong enough to be his partner.

"I could talk to her," Caleb said.

"No! Dad, I'll work something out. First, I have to stick it out for a month."

Caleb snorted with laughter. "Like you're worried about being able to keep the job. Son, you're the best!"

With a wry grin, Logan said, "Thanks, Dad. But promise you won't say anything to Abby."

"All right, all right. I'll bide my time. But, son, if you find a place that's right, I'll make sure you can afford it."

Logan appreciated his father's offer. In fact, his throat tightened at the support. But he didn't know what he would do. Except stick as close to Abby as he could.

When they reached the barn and dismounted, rubbing down their horses, Ellen came running from the house. Floyd abandoned his horse for a hug from his wife.

Logan stepped closer. "Ellen? Is everything all right?"

"Everything's fine. We're all back except for Jed and Beth. The doctor wanted to keep her one more day to be sure she's okay, then they'll be home."

Floyd nodded to Logan. "Go on up to the house and report to Abby. She'll be anxious to hear how things are. We'll take care of the horses."

Logan muttered his thanks and hurried to the house, fighting himself to avoid breaking into a trot.

When he reached the kitchen, Abby was standing there. Without breaking stride, Logan wrapped his arms around her.

"Logan!" she exclaimed, shock in her voice.

He forced himself to back off, to turn her lose. "Sorry. I—we were all glad to hear everything's all right."

"You talked to Ellen? She was anxious to see Floyd." Abby avoided his gaze, but at least she was talking to him.

"Uh, yeah. Floyd said to report to you because you'd be worried about everything."

"Yes, I intended for us to start the roundup today. Maybe we can pull everything together to start tomorrow."

"We started today."

"But you were shorthanded!" she exclaimed.

He explained how they'd taken care of that problem.

"That's wonderful, Logan. Thank you. I couldn't have managed as well."

"Yes, you could have. But now we have enough people to finish up without you having to work so hard. It will give you time to help Beth settle in."

She opened her mouth to protest, then frowned. "Maybe you're right. Beth will be back tomorrow. Rob and I talked about making sure everything's taken care of at their place before Jed returns. Maybe I will accept your offer."

Logan smiled. "Good. Beth and the baby's health is more important than a bunch of cows."

"Yes, but…but Logan, what happened just now… and the other night…I can't—"

"I got carried away. I promise not to do that unless it's what you want, okay? I like it here. I want to stay." He held his breath, waiting for her answer.

Abby gave a big sigh. "I'd like you to stay."

Logan almost broke out into a sweat as relief filled him. "I'll move into the manager's house after we finish the roundup."

Abby nodded without saying anything.

"Uh, we've got some extra mouths to feed tonight. Mom promised to make sure there was enough food."

"Your mother has been wonderful. She prepared most of it over at Melissa's. She wants you and your dad to join them there for dinner, but she and Melissa and Lindsay are bringing over the food for the hands."

Logan's jaw squared. "Where are you eating?"

"Here, of course."

"Then I'll eat here, too."

"Logan, your parents are going home after dinner. Lindsay, too. You should eat with them."

He studied Abby's face, trying to determine if his mother had insulted her in any way, or made any remarks about eating with the ranch hands. But Abby seemed okay.

"All right, since they're leaving. But I'd prefer to eat here."

She nodded without saying anything else about it. "Please tell the men dinner will be ready as soon as they wash up."

As he reluctantly turned to go, the back door opened and his mother and sister, along with Melissa, entered, their hands full.

"Son, you're back! Where's your father?"

Logan stepped forward and took the large pot his mother carried before he bent to kiss her cheek. "He's at the barn."

"You'll both come to Melissa's for dinner, of course."

He nodded. "We'll be there in a few minutes." Then he hurried out of the house, with a last look at Abby.

Abby got up early the next morning to help Ellen cook for the expanded crew. But for the first time since she arrived on the ranch as a scrawny twelve-year-old, she wasn't going out to work with them.

Only school had interfered with her work even then. Aunt Beulah had insisted she attend class, even when she hadn't seen the importance of it. At twelve, her vision hadn't been as clear as it now was.

Today, she intended to go to Jed's place and make sure everything was squared away for their return.

Her manager would take care of everything. She could leave the roundup to Logan.

Which didn't explain why she held her breath until he appeared.

He strode into the kitchen, his large, muscular body exuding energy. Abby warmed as his gaze immediately sought her out, just as hers did him.

"Morning," he said with a smile.

"Morning. Why don't you take my chair this morning."

"Where are you going to eat?"

"Ellen and I are going to serve. We'll eat after you're in the saddle."

"We can serve ourselves. You need to—"

"Don't go thinking you're in charge just because I'm letting you run the roundup," Abby muttered so no one could hear.

"But, Abby—"

"Sit down so everyone else will. Breakfast is ready." She turned her back on him and crossed to the stove where Ellen was scooping up fluffy scrambled eggs.

She turned back to the table, pleased to discover Logan in her chair, the other men settling in around him. She leaned over to place a plate on the table next to him and felt a hand on her back. She whipped upright and stared at him.

"I was afraid you might lose your balance," he assured her.

She glared at him and moved back to the stove. The next time she approached the table, it was beside Floyd.

Half an hour later, the men had eaten and cleared out, leaving a lot of empty dishes in their wake. Abby helped Ellen start the cleaning up process.

How things had changed.

Two weeks later, Logan headed for the manager's house to clean up after a long day in the saddle. The air felt colder tonight. They were into November now, with Thanksgiving fast approaching.

And he was making no progress.

Oh, the ranch work was going well. He loved the place.

But he was no closer to Abby than he'd been the first day. She watched him. She even smiled at him now. But they kept a boss-employee relationship.

He'd gotten desperate, asking for conferences about things he'd never hesitated to take care of before. He'd even begun showing her a computer program in the evenings. They were spending a lot of time together. He felt as if they'd come to know each other well.

But he hadn't changed his mind about her. When their fingers would accidentally touch on the keys, he'd have to jerk away before he pulled her into his arms.

He was giving more and more thought to what his dad had said. As long as he was the employee, it was going to be impossible to take their relationship any further. And he was getting impatient.

But he didn't want to quit.

Maybe he could ask to invest in their operations, become a partner. But if he did that, and then Abby made it clear she didn't want any closer relationship, what would he do?

Hang around hoping she'd change her mind?

The phone interrupted his thoughts.

"Hello?"

"Crawford?"

He didn't recognize the rusty voice. "Yeah?"

"This is Pritchard. Neighbor to the Prine place. Remember me?"

"Yeah, I do." Who could forget the man?

"I need to talk to you. Can you come to dinner?"

"Tonight?" Logan asked, wondering what was going on.

"Yeah."

"Okay."

"Good. Don't tell that Kennedy woman you're coming. It's none of her business." Then he hung up the phone.

Chapter Twelve

Abby stared at herself in the mirror. She wasn't sure she had the nerve to show up at the dinner table like this. She was wearing jeans, of course, but she had topped her jeans with a blue sweater that clung in all the right places.

More radical was her hair. When she'd showered, she'd shampooed her hair and blown it dry. But instead of her traditional braid, she'd pulled the top and sides back and pinned them with a gold barrette. The rest of her hair hung down her back.

She blushed as she imagined Logan's reaction. He'd mentioned several times how much he wanted her to wear her hair loose. The only other time she'd had it loose, when they'd come together in the bathroom, he'd kissed her senseless.

Her lips curved into a sensual smile that she almost didn't recognize. And it wasn't because she was wearing lip gloss, either. She'd begun adding that a week ago.

And mascara. Even a little blush.

She loved the way Logan's eyes lit up when he saw her. And nowadays, she had more time to spend on her grooming. To urge Logan to show a greater interest.

Of course, she'd told him not to kiss her again as long as he worked for her. And she was beginning to think firing him was the only thing that would change the situation.

And it might be worth it.

She was hungry for his kisses.

The sound of the dinner gong awakened her from her thoughts. She hurried down the stairs, anxious to be there when Logan entered.

"My, don't you look nice," Ellen said, beaming at her from the stove as she entered the kitchen.

"Thanks," Abby murmured, smiling. Ellen knew what she was up to. So why couldn't Logan figure it out?

Floyd came back in from ringing the gong and did a double-take. "My, my, Abby, you look beautiful."

"Thanks, Floyd." She appreciated the compliments, but she wasn't going to all this trouble for Floyd.

The back door opened and the men began filing in. Barney came first and then Dirk. And then no one.

Logan must be running late. Though disappointed, Abby turned to help Ellen put the food on the table, sure he'd appear any minute.

Barney and even Dirk complimented her on her appearance. She thanked them but her gaze kept returning to the door.

"Well, I guess we're ready to eat," Ellen announced and pulled out her chair.

"But where's Logan?" Abby asked.

"Oh, sorry, I forgot to tell you. He called and said he wouldn't be here for dinner. He had something come up." Ellen began passing dishes around the table.

Abby felt like crying. "Oh. Maybe I should take him some leftovers later."

"I offered, but he said he'd be eating out."

Jealousy shafted through Abby. Eating with whom? Logan was an attractive man. That was a ridiculous understatement, she admitted to herself. Women stared at him when he went into town. Not only was he handsome, but he was also strong, dynamic and charming. Hardworking. Intelli—

"Abby? Don't you want some potatoes?" Floyd asked, patiently holding a dish of whipped potatoes in his hands.

"Yes, of course. I'm starving." She piled food on her plate and then stared at it, as if she'd forgotten what it was for.

The men began their usual chitchat about work that day, and Abby half-listened, but mostly she thought about Logan and where he could be.

Some ladies in the area didn't hesitate to invite a man to dinner. Had some widow offered a home-cooked meal as enticement to Logan? Or had he asked a lady to dinner?

Abby felt sick to her stomach at the thought. He

acted as if he was interested in her. His eyes told her he wanted to get closer.

But he never did.

She didn't think it was because his mother disapproved. She called on a regular basis and talked to Abby about her family. She even asked for Abby's opinion about Lindsay and her dissatisfaction with her family's restrictions.

With the ranch demanding less of Abby's time, she was considering taking more classes at the university, learning about other things. She'd never give up ranchwork. It was important to her. But now she could have more.

Which brought her thoughts back to Logan.

More was what she wanted from him. She wanted him to court her, to touch her, to tell her he wanted her. Finally she admitted she wanted him to ask her to marry him, to make a family, to have babies. She wanted what her sisters had.

She'd begun in search of her dream after Aunt Beulah died, and had thought that dream was travel, freedom. Now she knew her dream was love and family.

With Logan.

"Are you going out tonight?" Ellen asked.

"What?" Abby returned, puzzled.

"Well, you're all fixed up. I thought maybe you had plans."

"No, I—"

The phone rang.

Abby leaped from her chair, sure it was Logan.

"Hi, it's Melissa."

"Hi, Melissa."

"Are you eating yet?"

"Yes, we just started."

"Well, could you and Ellen and Floyd come over after dinner? I've made a special dessert and I want you to try it."

"I don't—"

"Please, Abby? It's important."

She could never turn down such a plea from one of her sisters. "Of course. Is everything all right?"

"Everything's wonderful. We'll see you in a few minutes."

Now she had two things to worry about.

Though Ellen asked her about Melissa, she assured the housekeeper that everything was all right. But she kept the invitation quiet until Dirk and Barney left. Then she told the other two about Melissa's request.

The three of them walked over to Melissa and Rob's in silence. Abby noted that the manager's house, where Logan now lived, was dark. He hadn't come home. She checked her watch. It was seven-thirty. Not late.

Surely he'd be home soon.

When they reached her sister's house, they discovered that Jed and Beth were there also, a rare occasion since Beth stayed in bed most of the time.

"What are you doing here?" Abby asked.

"Jed said we should come. And I sure wasn't going to argue. I'm so tired of staring at the wallpaper I'm about to go crazy," Beth replied.

"Want me to have the wallpaper changed?" Jed asked, concern coloring his voice.

Beth rolled her eyes. "No, sweetie, I don't."

Melissa began passing around coconut pie, assisted by Terri and Wayne. Rob had corralled the other four children and was keeping them entertained.

"I really don't want any," Abby said, trying to smile. How could she think about pie when Logan was out with another woman? She was positive that that was the case.

"You have to eat some, Abby," Melissa urged. "And Terri's bringing you a cup of coffee. Don't worry, it's decaf. I know Beth can't have any other kind."

Beth and Abby exchanged a glance. Then Abby looked at Rob. He was beaming.

"I think we need to get to the announcement," she said, sitting up straight.

"Does everyone have something to drink?" Melissa asked, ignoring Abby.

"Yes, Mom," Terri answered. "And I agree with Aunt Abby. What's going on?"

"You don't know?" Abby asked, assuming the children would already know.

"No," Wayne answered. "They've been excited all afternoon, but they wouldn't tell us anything."

Rob stood. "Well, we wanted all the family together before we did. But since we're all here, I think it's time. Right, Melissa?"

She crossed the room and clasped Rob's hand. "Yes, it's time." She drew a deep breath. Then, she said, "Beth's not the only one in this room who's pregnant."

Abby and Beth realized her meaning at once. Mary Ann, who'd crossed the room to lean on Ellen's knee looked puzzled. "What does that mean? Are you going to have a baby, Grandma Ellen?"

"Land's sakes, no, dearie, but I think your mommy is."

The room erupted into celebration as everyone congratulated Rob and Melissa. Abby couldn't have been happier for them.

But it only pointed out the difference in her life and those of her sisters. She'd been hoping for marriage and family, thinking Logan was the man of her dreams.

Now he was out with someone else.

Later, back at home, she said good-night to Floyd and Ellen and headed for the stairs. But the phone stopped her.

Rob was on the line. "Heard something I thought I should pass on to you."

"What?"

"Well, you haven't been having any more trouble with Pritchard, have you?"

"No, of course not. I would've told you."

"A guy who works for Pritchard called me. He was wondering why your manager was having dinner with Pritchard tonight."

When Abby said nothing, he asked, "Logan wasn't home for dinner, was he?"

"No, he wasn't."

"There's probably some logical explanation for it, Abby, but I thought you should be aware. I don't think Logan would betray you in any way, but— well, I don't know what's going on."

"Neither do I."

She hung up the phone and stood staring into space.

"Abby?" Ellen said, touching her arm. "Is everything all right?"

"Everything's fine," she managed to say with a weak smile. "Good night."

In her bedroom, she stared out the window at the manager's house, still dark. Why would Logan have dinner with Pritchard?

Of course, the good news was he wasn't with a woman, as she'd feared.

Instead he was with the enemy.

The next morning, Logan ran late to breakfast on purpose. He didn't want any extra time with Abby. He'd be too tempted to tell her his news.

But he couldn't. Not yet.

He'd learned long ago not to count on something until all the papers had been signed. His father's lawyer was working on it and thought they'd have everything tied up in a week.

One week.

Then he could tell her. Then he could kiss her. Then he wouldn't be her employee anymore.

"Sorry I'm late," he said as he came in, his gaze going first to Abby, sitting in her normal place.

"Late night?" she asked, a challenge in her gaze.

Uh-oh. She wasn't happy with him. Did she think he'd had a date? The idea amused him. She couldn't think that. He'd practically drooled over her ever since he'd arrived.

"Nope. Just slow moving this morning." He grinned at her, but she stared at him, no response on her face. His grin faded as he realized she was seriously miffed.

Floyd broke the tension. "You gonna tell the guys?" he asked Abby.

She stared at him blankly before she nodded. "Yes, of course. Melissa announced last night that she's expecting."

Barney whooped in excitement and even Dirk grinned.

Logan added his congratulations. Immediately his mind looked to the future. If he and Abby worked things out, maybe Beth and Melissa wouldn't be alone in producing babies.

A soft smile settled on his lips until his gaze met Abby's.

He'd better worry about the present, he decided.

When they finished eating, he was surprised that Abby rose also.

"You riding out with us today? We don't really need you," he said.

"Yes, you do. I've changed the assignments. I want you to check on the pump at the well on the back side of the property. I'll be Floyd's partner riding fence. Dirk and Barney will form the other team."

"The pump's not working?" As far as he knew, no one had been out there to check, so how had she found out that it was broken?

"I'm not sure. A neighbor flew over that pasture recently, and he thought it looked dry. I thought you could check it and see what the status is."

Her story didn't sound right, but he could be wrong. "Sure, I can do that." Then he gave her a special smile. "Sure you don't want to ride with me?"

"No."

No smile. No warmth. No interest.

He wanted to talk to her alone, find out what was going on, but she stuck to Floyd like glue. When Ellen offered to pack him a sandwich, he stayed behind the others and tried to pump Ellen.

"What's wrong with Abby?"

"I don't know what you mean," Ellen said, keeping her gaze fixed on the sandwich she was making.

Logan gave a gusty sigh. "Yes, you do, but I'm not surprised you're being loyal to Abby. But I can't fix what's wrong unless I know what it is."

"I reckon she'll tell you when she wants you to know."

He took his sandwich with a thank-you and headed for the barn.

It was the longest week of his life. Everything that could go wrong had. Abby had sent him on every fool's errand she could find.

And she'd kept her distance.

No more conferences. No more private discussions about the ranch. No more computer lessons.

Just coldness.

The lawyer called Thursday afternoon to tell him to be in his colleague's office in Tumbleweed at nine o'clock the next morning to close on the sale. Logan decided to wait to tell Abby until the next morning. The less time she had to think about all of it, the more surprised she'd be.

He hoped it was a happy surprise.

But he was beginning to have his doubts.

The next morning, he told her he had a family emergency and needed the morning off. Though she gave him a sharp look, she finally agreed.

In Tumbleweed, he shook Pritchard's hand, after signing the papers to purchase his ranch. The man handed over the keys to the padlock on the front gate and to the house and outbuildings, each one labeled.

"Pleasure doing business with you," Pritchard muttered without a smile and stalked out of the office.

He'd offered his ranch to Logan, thinking perhaps his father might want to purchase it. But he'd sworn he'd never sell it to Abby or any of her family because she'd accused him of cutting the fences. Logan had leaped at the opportunity, calling his father at once to ask him to back him on the purchase.

Now he could go to Abby with connecting land that would enhance the Circle K operations. They would be on an equal footing. And if she needed time to accept his offer…or him…he'd be nearby to keep reminding her how much he loved her.

After Pritchard's departure, he shook hands with the two lawyers and hurried to his truck. He couldn't wait to tell Abby. It had gone against the grain to keep the secret from her.

Lunch was almost over when he got to the house.

"There's plenty left, Logan," Ellen assured him.

Abby didn't speak to him.

"I might eat something in a minute, Ellen, thanks, but first I need to speak to Abby."

She stared at him, saying nothing.

"In private," he added.

* * *

It was almost as if she could read his mind. He was going to quit.

Not that she blamed him. She'd been hateful to him this week. But he shouldn't have betrayed her, gone over to Pritchard's side. She hadn't figured out his angle, yet, or Pritchard's, either. But the fact that he'd kept his meeting with Pritchard secret told her he was hiding something.

Without speaking, she stood and headed for her office, knowing he'd be right behind her. She only hoped she could remain stoic until he'd gone.

It wouldn't be easy.

She'd shed her share of tears late at night during the past week.

Rounding the desk, she sat down in her chair and waited.

Logan placed his fists on the desk and leaned toward her. "Abby, I'm resigning."

She pressed her lips together. When she thought she had her voice under control, she said, "Going to work for Pritchard, are you?"

She could tell she'd shocked him. He straightened, his eyes widening. Then he grinned. "Nope. Why would you think that?"

"I know you met with him last week."

He grinned even more. "So why didn't you ask me what I was doing?"

"What you do in the evenings is your business."

Suddenly he acted as if a lightbulb had been illuminated in his head. "Abby Kennedy, that's why you've been mad at me all week! Did you think I was doing something I shouldn't? Surely you didn't think I'd side with that man on anything when it came to you?''

A small glimmer of hope began to rise until she remembered he'd resigned. "It was possible," she said, ducking her head.

"Nope. It wasn't." He strode around the desk, taking Abby by surprise. She reared back in her chair, trying to protect herself.

He took her arms and pulled her from the chair into his embrace. She struggled against him. He didn't hurt her, but he didn't let her get away, either.

"Don't you want to know why I'm resigning?" he asked, his face very close to hers.

"I—I assume you got a better offer." Maybe a more accommodating boss, someone who wouldn't object to his kisses.

One big hand slid beneath her chin to force her gaze to his. "I'm getting my own place."

"Oh! Oh, well, congratulations, Logan. I'm sure—that's wonderful news." She should be happy for him. He'd do very well on his own. But she didn't want him to go. She didn't want... "Where?"

He grinned. "Think about it."

Suddenly everything clicked into place. "Pritchard? You're buying Pritchard's place? I didn't even know it was for sale. We would've—you got in ahead of us without even saying anything!" she accused, her voice rising.

"He refused to even consider selling to you. He was mad about the fence thing. Decided to retire since he couldn't expand."

"We could've outbid you!"

"It wouldn't have mattered, Abby."

She pulled from his arms and paced around the office.

"Damn! We'd talked about maybe, someday— Now we can't expand like we'd hoped." Suddenly she whirled to stare at him. "How much do you want?"

"That's my girl! I knew you wouldn't be a quitter."

Her gaze narrowed. "Is that what you're doing? Hoping to turn a quick profit?" She stepped over to the desk. "Okay, how much?"

"It's a steep price."

He grinned, and Abby wanted to slap him. How dare he torment her like this. Didn't he know how much he had caused her to suffer already? She could hardly sleep at night, and her heart was breaking. "How much?" she demanded, her voice cracking with the stress.

Walking around the desk until he reached her side, he lifted a hand and caressed her cheek. "Your heart," he whispered. "That's all I'm asking."

Abby's knees were shaking and she was afraid to think he meant what she'd been longing for for so long. "My...heart? What do you mean?"

"Sweetheart," he said as he wrapped his arms around her, "I've been crazy about you ever since I arrived. I can't keep my hands off you any longer. If you need more time, you can have it, as long as I can do this," he said, then covered her lips with his.

Oh, yes! Abby's spirit made a miraculous recovery from the sickness it had been suffering the past week. She slid her arms around his neck, feeling as if she'd come home at last.

"And this," he murmured as he lifted his lips from hers to trace a trail down her neck.

"Yes, please," she agreed before seeking his lips again. She hadn't had enough. She wasn't sure she'd ever have enough.

"I lied," he finally confessed after an incredible kiss.

Shock filled Abby. "You did?" she cried.

"Yeah. It's not just your heart I want. I want your hand in marriage. I want a lifetime with you. I want your babies. Am I asking too much?"

She collapsed against him. "Oh, no! But—but I'm not like your mother."

"I know," he assured her with a grin. "But Mom says I'll be an idiot if I don't marry you."

"She did?"

"Oh, yeah. And Dad was all for it when they came down here after I'd been here four days."

"He was?" Exultation filled Abby.

"He was," he assured her and emphasized it by kissing her again.

Several minutes later, they came up for air again. "Sweetheart, if we don't stop this, I'm going to anticipate our wedding vows over there on that couch," Logan warned.

"Okay," Abby happily agreed.

Logan reared back, shock on his face. Then he stepped away from her.

"What's wrong?" Abby asked, suddenly worried.

"Was I wrong? I thought you were a virgin."

"Does my answer affect your proposal?" she asked frostily, not liking his question.

"Hell, no, but it'll affect what happens now."

"Then it's none of your business," she said, her nose in the air.

He pulled her against him. "Abby, I don't want to...you've waited this long. You might be afraid—"

"The only thing I'm afraid of is snakes, and I've found my hero who'll protect me. So I'm not afraid, Logan. I'll never be afraid of you." She soundly kissed him.

He pulled back, grinning. "Sweetheart, you'll never have to ask twice. Let me lock the door."

Abby waited impatiently, eager to greet her dream. There were babies to be made, a family to love.

While she waited for Logan's arms to hold her, she said a silent prayer of thanks for Aunt Beulah, for her wisdom, her warm heart, and the future she gave to all three sisters.

Logan pulled her against him. "We're getting married as soon as we can get a license."

"Your mother will complain."

"I know," he agreed with a grin. "But since I didn't bring any condoms with me, I think I can convince her that we don't need to waste time."

"I love the way you think," Abby told him.

"Abby Kennedy soon-to-be Crawford, I love everything about you."

Perfect words to fulfill Abby's dream.

Epilogue

Sunday evening on the Circle K meant the family gathered for their weekly meal. Abby, Melissa and Beth took turns hosting the dinner, each with the help of her housekeeper.

Tonight, Beth's five-month-old son was letting everyone know he wanted his dinner *now*. Jed hurried to warm a bottle in the bottle warmer.

"Isn't he handy?" Beth asked her sisters, a teasing grin on her face.

"Thank goodness, or we'd all be deaf," Abby said, smiling, too. "Little Jason has the best lungs in the county."

"If our baby takes after Terri, we'll be entering that competition," Rob said.

"Dad!" Terri protested. She was helping Ellen set the table. Dinner wasn't ready yet, but the entire family was gathered in the kitchen.

Mary Ann leaned against Rob's knee, her fear of

men long forgotten. "Our baby will cry?" she asked, worry on her little face.

Rob hauled her into his lap and dropped a kiss on her head. "Sure, our baby will cry. Babies don't know how to talk. That's how they ask for a bottle."

Mary Ann leaned over to where Melissa sat beside Rob and patted her mother's big tummy. "I'll teach our baby to talk 'cause I can talk good. Mommy said."

"Yes, you can, sweetie," Melissa agreed.

Everyone laughed. Then Ellen declared dinner was ready. Abby and Terri began to help her put it on the table. Jed gave Beth the warm bottle, which she promptly stuck into the baby's mouth, and peace descended over the group.

When everyone was seated at the table, Logan, at the head of the table, tapped on his glass with his knife. "Before we start eating, Abby has an announcement to make."

"Yes," Abby agreed, smiling at Logan, then looking at their large family. "I wanted to tell you that we're adding to the family."

There were several exclamations and the beginnings of questions, but Abby ignored everyone and kept going. "Lindsay was supposed to be here this weekend, but she got grounded again and couldn't come."

Beth and Melissa looked at each other. Then Melissa asked, "Lindsay is going to move in with you?"

"Oh, no," Abby said cheerfully, "but she was going to bring us a puppy. Logan's father's cowherd dog had puppies and he's sending us one."

"Abby!" Beth protested indignantly. "We thought you were going to tell us you're expecting! How could you be so cruel?"

Abby smiled at Logan again. Then she looked at her two sisters. "Oh, did I forget to mention that, too?"

Pandemonium broke out as everyone jumped up to congratulate both Abby and Logan.

"When?" Melissa asked.

"In about six months," Abby said. "Our babies will be six months apart if you have yours on schedule," she told Melissa. "After all, Jason will be six months old two days after your due date."

"And are you having a boy, too?" Rob asked. Melissa and Rob had discovered they were having a boy, which pleased Wayne and Billy. They said they needed a new brother to even the numbers.

Abby shrugged with a chuckle. "Logan's sure it's a girl. He's already arranging for ballet lessons."

Everyone burst into laughter, including Logan.

Several minutes later, with everyone seated, Abby spoke again. Lifting her tea glass, she said, "I want to make a toast to Aunt Beulah. She was a great lady, who left us her most precious treasure."

"You mean the money?" Jed asked, frowning.

"No, though I think we've put it to good use. No," Abby said, still smiling, "Aunt Beulah's most precious gift to us was her love. And we're doing a great job of passing it along."

Everyone lifted their glass, even Mary Ann, though she wasn't sure what was going on. "To Aunt Beulah," they chorused.

The three sisters tapped their glasses together and shared a smile. They were truly blessed.

* * * * *

Don't miss Judy Christenberry's next book in the Circle K series in October 2000, when Lindsay Crawford meets her match. Only in Silhouette Romance.

USA *Today* Bestselling Author

SHARON SALA

has won readers' hearts with thrilling tales
of romantic suspense. Now Silhouette Books
is proud to present five passionate stories from
this beloved author.

Available in August 2000:
ALWAYS A LADY
A beauty queen whose dreams have been dashed in a
tragic twist of fate seeks shelter for her wounded spirit
in the arms of a rough-edged cowboy....

Available in September 2000:
GENTLE PERSUASION
A brooding detective risks everything to protect the
woman he once let walk away from him....

Available in October 2000:
SARA'S ANGEL
A woman on the run searches desperately for a reclusive
Native American secret agent—the only man who can save
her from the danger that stalks her!

Available in November 2000:
HONOR'S PROMISE
A struggling waitress discovers she is really a rich heiress—
and must enter a powerful new world of wealth and
privilege on the arm of a handsome stranger....

Available in December 2000:
KING'S RANSOM
A lone woman returns home to the ranch where she was
raised, and discovers danger—as well as the man she once
loved with all her heart....

COMING NEXT MONTH

#1468 HIS EXPECTANT NEIGHBOR—Susan Meier
Storkville, USA

The *last* thing loner Ben Crowe wanted was a beautiful single woman renting the cottage on his ranch—and a pregnant one at that! Yet when Gwen Parker gave him her sweet smile, how could he refuse? And how could he guard his hardened heart?

#1469 MARRYING MADDY—Kasey Michaels
The Chandlers Request...

It was one week before Maddy Chandler's wedding to a safe, sensible man, and she should have been ecstatic. But then her former love Joe O'Malley suddenly moved in right next door, with plans to show lovely Maddy *he* was the groom for her!

#1470 DADDY IN DRESS BLUES—Cathie Linz

When Curt Blackwell went to check out his daughter's new preschool, he was surprised to find that her enticing teacher, Jessica Moore, was "Jessie the Brain" from their high school days! Suddenly Curt was looking forward to staying after school....

#1471 THE PRINCESS'S PROPOSAL—Valerie Parv
The Carramer Crown

Brains, beauty...a prize stallion—Princess Adrienne de Marigny had Hugh Jordan's every desire. And he had a little something *she* wanted. The princess's proposal involved a competition, winner take all. But the plan backfired, leading to a different proposal....

#1472 A GLEAM IN HIS EYE—Terry Essig

Johanna Durbin was on her own after helping raise her siblings—and intended to enjoy single life. That is, until she met sexy guardian Hunter Pace, who needed daddy lessons—fast! But was Hunter looking for a temporary stint...or a family forever?

#1473 THE LIBRARIAN'S SECRET WISH—Carol Grace

Tough, brooding, calloused—and devilishly handsome—investigator Nate Callahan was the kind of guy librarian Claire Cooper had learned to stay away from. Still, how could she turn her back on a missing little boy? Or on a chance to feel the love she'd always dreamed of...?